Uncle Sharif's Life in Music

to my dear Eric

you are missed so much —

Uncle Sharif's Life in Music

stories by

Kazim Ali

SIBLING RIVALRY PRESS
LITTLE ROCK, ARKANSAS
DISTURB / ENRAPTURE

Sibling Rivalry Press, LLC
PO Box 26147
Little Rock, AR 72221

info@siblingrivalrypress.com

www.siblingrivalrypress.com

ISBN: 978-1-943977-20-8

Library of Congress Control No. 2016945233

This title is housed permanently in the Rare Books and Special
Collections Vault of the Library of Congress.

First Sibling Rivalry Press Edition, October 2016

The italics on pages 232-233 are an English translation of the
lyrics of "Spem in Alium" by Thomas Tallis.

STORIES

UNCLE SHARIF'S LIFE IN MUSIC

When I was twelve years old there was a summer when it seemed like every Indian person who flew into the Buffalo airport just had to come to our place for dinner before they got back on a plane and flew wherever else they were really headed.

If we were *really* lucky then they just *had* to stay overnight and visit Niagara Falls the next day. I don't know if you have ever seen Niagara Falls but seriously: it's just water. A whole lot of water going really fast, I grant you, but in the end: just water.

Uncle Sharif and Aunty Zuleiqah came in between Pinky-Khala and Bubboo-Uncle at the beginning of the summer and Jamshad Khan and the Magic Moulana at the end of the summer. We always looked forward to Aunty Zuleiqah's visits because even though she was our mom's sort of older sister she listened to rock music and knew who ZZ Top and Huey Lewis and the News were and Uncle Sharif always brought his sitar, for which he had to buy a whole extra plane ticket. And unlike the other couples that visited us, Aunty Zuleiqah and Uncle Sharif did not have a ton of bratty kids we would then have to teach all of our made-up games to. And when it was time to say goodbye the crumpled bills they pressed into our hands were 20s or 10s not 5s.

Oh and there was one other reason we loved and were horrified by Uncle Sharif. As the rumor went, meaning we heard grown-ups talking in the kitchen downstairs by hiding on the landing of the staircase at two in the morning, Uncle Sharif was secretly a Hindu.

"That is what I am telling you, *na,*" exclaimed Pinky-Khala loud enough for us to hear even if we were in bed like we were supposed to be. "He doesn't even hide it, there is Krishna and Ganesh and whatever else you think hanging just there beside the door as soon as you walk into the apartment."

"But it's from his music, Pinky," our mom said, ever the peacemaker.

"Music, schmusic," declared Pinky-Khala. "He has even a Hindu name for when he goes to temple, I heard from our three-doors-down neighbor Abida." She paused for maximum dramatic effect. "*Shyam*. Shyam! From Sharif he makes Shyam, such a scandal it is, *taubah!*" And we heard the familiar sound of her palm slapping against her forehead.

My little sister Rubi started giggling on the landing. I put my hand on her mouth but she wouldn't stop and we had to run upstairs before anyone knew we were there.

The next morning, we were all out on the front lawn playing Statues. I don't know where we learned it from or if we just made it up but like all of our games it sort of didn't have a point. One person was the buyer and one person was the seller and everyone else was a Statue. The buyer would go back inside the house and get some of Mom's famous sweet mint lemonade. The seller would then take one of us by the hand to make a Statue. The seller would swing you around and around and around and when she let you go, you would spin around the yard like a lunatic and then freeze in your Statue shape.

"Okay, you can come out now," Rubi hollered in to my cousin Beeko. My other cousins and I littered the lawn like an exotic sculpture garden. I had decided to be a crazy monkey, my hands flung up in the air. Near me, my older brother Khaled was crawling on all fours. Tiger? Dog? And beyond him my cousin Dolly was sitting cross-legged in a yoga pose. Boring! I had this one in the bag.

Beeko came out with a bag of *chevda*, lifting fistfuls into his mouth and then licking his fingers and plunging them in for another bite. And of course none of us could move a muscle to get our share.

"Hello, mister," said Rubi in a booming man-voice. "Would you like to come into my Statue shop?"

Now the buyer and the seller walk around the lawn, looking

at all the different statues. The seller is supposed to describe and explain what each piece is. You are supposed to be realistic enough all the way down to your facial expression that the buyer would choose you. If the buyer chooses you then you become the new buyer, the buyer becomes the new seller and the seller rejoins the Statues.

It probably sounds like a dumb game now but back then all you wanted to do was be the new buyer so *you* could be the one doing the choosing. I was sure I would get chosen because I had the craziest expression of my face, plus my body was flung out like a real monkey. I wasn't just sitting there with my eyes closed like Dolly. Though my arms were starting to get tired. If you move, you lose.

Besides Khaled and Dolly, my only other competition was my know-it-all cousin Jonny, so called because his mom always called him "Afzal-*jaan*," which means "Afzal darling." Which kind of sucks because if anyone ever called me Zeffer darling I would get beat up. But Jonny's the star of the soccer team and convinced his mom to buy him an electric guitar so he can be in a rock band at school so even if anyone at school knew where his nickname came from it would probably just make it cool. Me, I have the same name as a dumb monkey from the "Babar" stories. "No *jaan*," my mother would comfort me, "also you are named after the *east wind*. You come so gently in the spring time to cheer everyone up after winter!"

Thanks, Ma. I'll just tell them that at school. I'm sure that will help.

At any rate, Jonny was making me sweat because he decided to be a Statue in the shape of a guy surfing. His arms were outstretched, his legs planted wide and he had a really cool expression on his face, like "I love the ocean. Don't you wish you were here?"

Water. Again. And me, scared of going in the deep end of the pool at the community center ever since I saw *Jaws*. Yes, I realize that it makes no sense but that's what "phobia" *means*, doesn't it? Irrational fear?

Of course I was sure I could beat a dumb surfer—I was a crazy monkey. Crazy is better than cool, right?

Beeko and Rubi were going from Statue to Statue. "And this little man," said Rubi stopping in front of me, "is a … weird … *dwarf.*"

"I'm not a dwarf, I'm a monkey!" I exclaimed, dropping the act.

"You broke the rules," sang Dolly. "You get disqualified." Jonny and Khaled were still frozen solid.

"No fair," I said.

"Fair is fair," she said flatly, folding her elbows and raising her chin.

Before our fight could finish, we were distracted by my dad's sky blue station wagon pulling into the driveway.

"Oh Uncle Sharif and Aunty Zuleiqah are here," exclaimed my sister, running off toward the car, followed by Dolly, Khaled and Jonny.

Beeko stayed beside me, watching, still reaching into his bag of fried crispy rice. "I would have picked you anyway," he said to me, patting me on the shoulder with a greasy hand.

"Thanks, Beek," I said glumly, plunging my hand in for some *chevda.* We walked over to the car together, where Aunty Zuleiqah in her pink georgette sari was dispensing chocolates and ten-dollar bills.

"Hello, *baccheh,*" she called out to us. "God, Beeko, stop eating that stuff, you're getting *fat.* And soon you'll be farting all evening long and none of us will have a moment's peace!"

Everyone laughed. Why is it Aunty Zuleiqah could say stuff like that and people would laugh but if I said it I would get a *chutki* on the inside of my forearm where they hurt the most?

At the trunk of the car my father and Uncle Sharif were delicately lifting out the red vinyl case that held my uncle's sitar.

"Oh yes, the *sitar,*" said Aunty Zuleiqah. "That too I had to give up my window seat for the box of wood!"

Uncle Sharif did not look the way I remembered him. He seemed quieter, older, a little slower. Even though I knew he was the same age as my dad and only a couple years older than Aunty Zuleiqah, he seemed much much older than that. As old as my grandfather.

"How are you, *behta?*" he asked me, his dry hand chucking my chin. I squirmed just so slightly away from him. He laughed. "Not friends anymore? It's all right. I've had a long trip." He took my mother's arm, less out of friendship I thought and more out of a need to lean on someone. As they walked ahead into the house I heard him say, "He's grown a lot since I've seen all of you last. How is everything?"

Aunty Zuleiqah and my father followed with the suitcases. She was saying, "It's hard for him, but we are trying our best to live with it. What else can we do?"

I felt cold as we walked into the house after them silently, even though I was still sweating from our game.

★

While my mom was scooping rice out of her giant pot with a small dish and serving everyone, Aunty Zuleiqah put a small plate in front of Uncle Sharif: a plum cut in wedges with a scoop of cottage cheese in the middle.

"Sorry Ruhi," she said to my mother, "but it's doctor's orders. No more Indian *salan* for him."

Uncle Sharif patted Aunty Zuleiqah's hand. "Not to worry, darling, I like this much more than spicy-spicy chicken!"

The plum looked really delicious to me. "Ma, I want a plum, too," I said.

Aunty Zuleiqah laughed. "Now, see, I've been here one day only and already I am ruining everyone's health!"

All the grown-ups laughed and as they were sitting down to dinner and my mom was making little plates for Rubi and Beeko, my Dad herded Khaled, me, Jonny and Dolly into the family room. "Look, kids," he said to us, "Uncle Sharif has had a long trip and needs to rest for a couple of days here. Try not to get too excited around him or cause too much commotion."

"You better tell Rubi and Beeko," I said. "They're the number one and number two commotion-causers!"

"I'll tell them," my Dad said, smoothing down my crazy monkey-hair. "Go in and eat."

★

Us kids were all sitting on the floor of the family room eating our food, a white sheet spread between us,

"What was *that* all about?" said Khaled, rolling his eyes.

"I don't know," I said. "Didn't Uncle Sharif look a lot older to you?"

"Well, he *is* older, dummy," said Dolly, flipping her hair and squinting at her nails. "Aunty Zuleiqah has orange nail polish. Do you think orange would look good on me?"

Rubi and Beeko started squealing with laughter. "Orange is an *old lady* color," said Rubi.

Dolly sniffed. "You don't know anything about what's stylish *now*, Rubi!"

"Do you think he knows how to play the guitar?" Jonny wondered out loud. "A guitar can't be *that* different than a sitar, can it?"

"It's *way* different," I said, even though I had no idea what a sitar was.

"No it's not," said Dolly. "You don't know *anything*."

"I do so," I said, my cheeks getting hot. "It's not the same. Ask him."

"I think it is the same," said Khaled, apologizing to me with his eyes. "Just that a guitar has six strings and a sitar has twelve. But I bet if you knew how to play a sitar it would be *easy-peasy* to play a guitar."

"Sweet. I'm going to bring my guitar tomorrow."

"He's not even going to like it, Jonny," I said. "He doesn't like rock and roll music, only Indian music."

But Jonny wasn't listening to me. He was pretending to play an air guitar while Beeko and Rubi clapped along.

Khaled grabbed my shoulder and stood up. "Come and help me with cleaning up or Mom is going to have a conniption."

I didn't even know what "conniption" meant but I knew what Mom looked like when she was having one.

"See you guys later," I mumbled, but no one was paying any attention to me.

★

I woke the next morning, just before dawn for *fajr* prayers. Usually my mom and dad were the only ones up that early. I went to the bathroom and splashed some water on my face and performed my *wadu* before going downstairs for prayers. As I walked past the prayer room, its slit of yellow light beneath the door, the voices of my parents chanting, I saw a figure outside on the patio in the dark.

I slipped through the kitchen and went out the french doors onto the patio. Sitting up on the wide wooden railing around the deck was Uncle Sharif, staring out into the darkness of the yard and singing a weird, wordless, tuneless note, sort of halfway between warbling and chanting a *sura*. "*Om bhur buva svah,*" he sang. I didn't recognize those words. Those were not any prayer I had been taught. I walked over and sat on the railing beside him. He turned to look at me and smiled but did not stop singing. "*Tat savitur varenyammmm.*" He turned back to the yard and sang some more. "*Bargo devasya deemahi...*"

His music made a weird space in my ear, mixed in with the crickets from the yard.

Inside the house, my parents' chanting stopped. It meant they had finished with the preliminary *duas* and were going to start the regular prayers. I looked back at the house and then back at Uncle Sharif. He was watching me, smiling. Still singing, he nodded, jerking his head back to the house, letting me know it was okay if I wanted to go. "*Dhiyo yo naaaa pracho daiyaaaat...*"

I turned back to the yard, pulled my knees up against my chest and rested my chin on them and closed my eyes.

As soon as I closed my eyes Uncle Sharif took it as a cue and started singing with words, but not more strange words like I was expecting. Instead he sang with the same weird tuneless tune, "Hey

Allah, Hey Allah, Allah, Allah, Hey Allah."

"You don't want to go in for prayers?" I asked him then.

"Oh no," he sang out, as if ordinary speaking was too flat for him. "I like to love God out here in the yard with the singing insects and the wet morning!"

"Are you a Muslim or a Hindu?" I asked him then. I guess I figured if no one else was around he might tell me.

Uncle Sharif laughed out loud. He turned around from the edge and eased himself back down to the deck. "Wouldn't *you* like to know?" he asked me jauntily and went back inside.

"That's not an answer," I muttered to myself in the dark.

★

Uncle Sharif was in the kitchen. He had turned only the little light above the stove on so everything was still dark. He was rummaging around in the fridge.

"Can I help you get something, Uncle Sharif?" I asked.

"*Hanh, behta, mujhse aapke mummy ke* 'special lemon juice' *chaye.*"

"Lemon juice?" I asked. I couldn't imagine drinking something so tart. Old Indian men are so weird.

"Yes, darling. Lemon juice, but I can't find it."

I reached past him to the inside of the fridge door where Mom kept the little plastic bottles shaped like lemons. "This stuff?" I asked.

His eyes lit up. "Yes, yes. Lemon juice. Pour me a glass, *jaan?*"

I shrugged. "Okay, if you want it." I got the smallest glass I could find from the cupboard and unscrewed the top of the lemon and squirted the juice until the glass was half-full of the tart stuff. "Here you go." Must be some kind of yoga healing thing, I figured.

Uncle Sharif sighed, appraising the glass and then gulped it down.

"Oh!" he cried out at once and then made for the sink, trying to spit it out. "That's not sweet at all," he said. And then he started laughing. "You tricked me!" he said, waggling a finger at me. "A good joke! You are a smart young man!"

He threw one arm around me and hugged me. Oh God. Lemon*ade*. He wanted Mom's special mint *lemonade*.

My mom charged into the kitchen then, her face alarmed, her bright orange prayer veil wrapped around her head so tightly it made her cheeks a little pudgy-looking. "What's all the commotion?" she demanded sharply. Then she saw Uncle Sharif and softened up right away. "Oh *bhai-jaan*," she wheedled in a musical tone, "I didn't know you were here. What do you need? Getting everything?"

"Oh yes, yes, Ruhi. My little nephew is helping me with *everything* I need." He shot me a sidelong glance and winked.

"All right then," she said in that same sing-songy voice, smiling sweetly at him, and a split second later shooting me a dangerous and accusing look—What? I didn't even *do* anything!—and then disappeared back down the hall.

"Quite a witty fellow you are," Uncle Sharif said, still laughing, wiping his eyes. "Tricked me pretty well, didn't you? Teach me to skip my prayers, ha!" And he clapped me on the shoulder. Hard. Ouch.

But I wasn't being witty, I thought to myself sadly. Just stupid. Like always.

"Good night now," he said walking down the hall. "Or good morning. Whatever God wills." He was still laughing as he walked up the stairs. "Good joke! Hey Allah, you listening? That one is my number one favorite nephew!"

Oh great. Me and Uncle Sharif. What a team.

★

We were supposed to leave for Niagara Falls an hour before lunch so we would have time to go to the botanical gardens and look at the floral clock before we had our picnic. The floral clock I had seen before but who could get tired of Mom's sandwiches—tuna and *nimbu achchar*, curried turkey and *mango achchar* and if we were really lucky cheddar cheese and hot mustard. Mom was in the kitchen making a whole bucket of them and of course Beeko and Rubi were in there too making their favorite kinds: for Rubi it

17

was called an "air sandwich"—two pieces of bread with nothing inside while Beeko favored the "bread sandwich." I guess you can imagine what was inside that. And for dessert? I can't swear by it but I believe it was Rubi that invented the famous "bread ball," where you take a pillowy slice of white bread, strip the crust off and roll it up into—yes, really—a little marble-sized ball.

Aunty Zuleiqah was painting Dolly's nails orange so I went into Uncle Sharif's bedroom where he was tuning his sitar. It whined and whined and he seemed lost in concentration, his eyes closed, waggling his head from side to side. I didn't want to disturb him so I sat down on the floor, half hidden by the ajar door.

Then he opened his mouth and started singing. I guess singing is the wrong word for it because there weren't any words. "Aaaaa'aaaaah," he crooned. Can you hum with your mouth open? And why do Indian songs all sound like they are out of tune? And that's when I realized he wasn't tuning his sitar; he was *playing* it.

He had a little metal thimble on one finger and he strummed while he sang. "And you?" he sang out. "Do you want to learn the sitar?"

"I couldn't," I said. "I'm no good with musical instruments. That's Jonny."

"You can play to God every day if you wanted," he sang, still waggling his head.

"Not really," I said slowly, trying to make him understand. "I can't even play the guitar and it only has six strings—how would I ever learn *twelve?*"

Then he stopped singing and opened his eyes and looked right at me. The weird whining music of the sitar continued. It sounded like there were three of him playing. Maybe that's why all the Hindu statues had six arms.

"There *are* twelve strings," he told me, "but you only play *two of them.*"

I watched his hands then. As one hand moved up and down the fretboard of the sitar, the index finger of the other, capped with the little metal thimble, barely flickered across the strings. And the room felt drenched in music.

"How does all that sound come out of two little strings?" I asked in wonder.

"Ah yes," he crooned, chuckling, closing his eyes once more and playing even louder. "That is a good question about both music and about praying to God."

God again? What is it with this guy?

Then Jonny came in, hefting his guitar case. "Sorry I'm late, Uncle Sharif. My dad couldn't drop me off until right now."

As usual, Jonny has *perfect* timing. Right when I was finally about to get some answers.

"Oh hey Zeff, are you going to learn how to play music today as well?"

I wanted to say yes but the last thing I wanted was to be stupid and useless in front of Jonny.

Uncle Sharif was looking out the window at the cottonwood trees shedding their little fluffy seeds.

"No," I said, getting up and making space for Jonny to come inside. I looked back at Uncle Sharif wanting him to ask me to stay or at least be sad I was leaving but he was lost in the movement of the drifting seeds.

★

Lucky for us the sun was out and Bubboo-Uncle had made his special carrot *halwa*. The clock's not so bad I guess. At least it tells the right time. We couldn't see the falls but we could *hear* it thundering in our ears and we could *feel* it on our skin.

Uncle Sharif had continued his long and honored tradition of weirdness by singing the whole way there in the car. Even when he didn't have anything to sing about he would look out the window at the street signs and sing. "Re-e-e-d Lobsterrrrrrrrr! Lewiston-Porter Roa-oa-oadddd." As if that wasn't bad enough Khaled, Dolly and Jonny all went with Pinky-Khala and Bubboo-Uncle so I got stuck crammed in with Beeko and Rubi who of course just thought Uncle Sharif was a genius and had to sing along with him at every note.

Do you know how weird the world is when everything is sung? But with no instruments. And no music.

Khaled, Dolly and Jonny ran off to Three Sisters Islands and Beeko and Rubi sat with the adults, starving for their sandwiches. I stood, watching the hands of the floral clock slowly turn.

"You have been to the Falls one million times I think," said Uncle Sharif, coming up beside me.

"Something like that," I said.

"And every time you look at it and you wonder, 'What's the big deal?'"

I laughed. "Sometimes, I guess."

He leaned over to me a little bit. "Why didn't you stay and learn music with your cousin this morning?" he whispered.

I looked at my hands. "I'm no good," I said.

"In Indian music," he said, "there is one note that changes and one note that stays the same. Which one do you think *you* are?"

"The one that stays the same?" I asked.

He leaned even closer, smiling. I could see his orange-stained teeth, smell the *paan parag* on his breath. "Wrong answer," he whispered.

★

After sandwiches we walked in a group toward the Falls. All around me, people moving. I felt lost in the group. I was a single note in a huge chattering family and no one seemed to stop talking long enough for me to say anything. Whenever I tried to speak I would have to shout to be heard over Khaled, Dolly, whoever.

Only Uncle Sharif floated along, like a ghost, completely silent now, his head swaying side to side. Strange a little, how in the silence of the car he felt compelled to sing and now, with the roaring of both voices and water everywhere and he clams up.

The roar of the water got louder and louder and our skin got wetter and wetter. Uncle Sharif got quieter and quieter. I watched his face. He *was* older than before, so much older. And then he opened eyes and looked at me. He opened his mouth and I thought he was going to say something but instead slowly, right there in the middle of the walk, he sank down to his knees.

It was so weird that I thought for a moment he was making a prayer to the water but then Aunty Zuleiqah screamed. Uncle Sharif sagged over to the side, but by that time my father was next to him and caught him. Everyone was screaming then but me, I think. My throat closed completely and I sank down to my knees as well. Uncle Sharif was still looking at me, his breathing hoarse.

I crawled over next to him. He was lying down now, his head on my father's lap.

"Don't be scared," he said. I blinked away the rain.

I don't know how so much time passed but suddenly around us people had arrived to help. There were paramedics and they were putting a mask on his face.

"Sing me something," he muttered to me, as the mask filled up with his breath.

"What?" I asked. "I don't know what to sing."

"Don't ask," he said. "Don't speak. Just sing. Don't think. Just sing."

"I don't know what to si-i-ing," I chirped out in the same warbly tuneless notes I had heard him use. "Unless you want me to sing about the wa-a-a-a-terrrr…"

He smiled behind the plastic mask and reached for my hand as they lifted him onto the stretcher. He reached toward me. I took his hand. It was dry, dry as wood, and he was pressing something into my palm. A tiny metal box, maybe three quarters of an inch square.

He said something behind the mask. I strained to hear him. "Keep this for me," he said, "Until I come back."

He said something else as they wheeled the stretcher down the path toward the ambulance but I only knew what it was by the outline of the word as his mouth pronounced it: *sing*.

Pinky-Khala went with them in the ambulance since she is a doctor and my mom and Aunty Zuleiqah began running toward the parking lot for Mom's car. I ran after them. After a little while they had to slow down and walk quickly. Aunty Zuleiqah took my hand.

"What did he give you, *behta?*"

I showed her the little box. She took it from me and pried it open. Inside there was what looked like red powder. My mom was getting into the car. Aunty Zuleiqah dipped one finger into the box and then touched me on my brow bone between my eyes. She handed the box back to me.

"Now say a prayer for him," she whispered.

"*Bismillah-hir-Rahman-nir-Raheem,*" I began to recite as I had been taught.

"Not that kind," she called over her shoulder as she got into the car. "The other kind!"

The Hindu kind? Is that what she meant? But I didn't remember the words he had said and I didn't want to get in trouble anyhow.

"Dear God in the sky," I croaked out tunelessly the way Uncle Sharif had on the car ride over, not noticing my father and uncle and the others coming up behind me. "Dear one in water," I continued, trying my hardest to dream up words. I opened my mouth and it filled with the water, water everywhere in the air. I could see Rubi staring at me. She was crying. I kept singing, my mouth filling with water, "I am Zeffer, Zeffer in the wi-i-i-nd, I am Zeffer the wind…"

And then I felt Rubi's little hand taking mine.

I was not frozen anymore, but being spun in wide circles by some unknown music in space. With Uncle Sharif's red powder glistening wetly on my forehead like a miner's lamp, Rubi's little sliding notes joining mine, I opened my mouth wide to the rain and infinite sky and sang.

SCREWDRIVER

- 1 -

Alex is dizzy from the third glass of gin and cold in the Buffalo winter, frost on the dark green grass, broken glass on the pavement. He has four more cigarettes left in the crumpled packet and seven dollars in his pocket to last until Friday.

The moon's orange, he thinks, the bus is coming, but if I spend money on the ride then I can't get an egg for breakfast tomorrow.

Hey Alex, says someone coming up the sidewalk. Dimitra.

Dimitra, do you have a cigarette.

His fingers are so cold when he touches her hands. Her hands on his hands, rolling her thumb on the lighter. He pulls mint into his mouth.

Jesus, he says, I hate these.

She puts her lighter in her purse and pulls out a plastic thermos to drink.

What's that.

Screwdrivers, she says. On account of us being at war I am now allowed to drink in public.

Screwdrivers.

I need my vitamins, she says. She sits down on the bench next to him. Another bus goes by.

Where are you getting to, he says, putting his hand on her leg. Above the knee, too high above the knee, he thinks.

She turns her thigh slightly out while she smokes. Home. I am a retail slave. I serve twisted gods. Work is rot, she says. Alex, your hand is on my leg.

Why didn't William pick you up from work.

Half my money goes to school and the other half goes to the government to pay for what.

The war, says Alex, taking his hand off her leg.

William is at home cooking me dinner. Finally a night off from the bar and he stays home to cook me dinner.

You got a good man.

Yeah. She stands. Alex, it's cold, you should go home.

They turned off my power. Can I have a screwdriver.

She hands him the thermos.

- 2 -

He is lying in bed with Joel when the phone rings.

I am going to kill you, says William.

Hello. Who the fuck is this.

It's William. I know you fucked Dimitra.

Jesus, says Alex, trying to sit up without disturbing the cover, his chest and stomach still slick from Joel.

I am going to punch you in the mouth—

Hey, says Alex, throwing the covers back and getting up.

William starts crying and Alex sits down on the edge of the bed.

Who is it, asks Joel.

I hate you, William says. I want to punch you in the face.

William, says Alex.

Don't hang up, says William. I don't have anyone to talk to. Fuck.

What does William want at one in the morning, Joel asks sitting up.

William, I don't know what you're talking about.

I read her journal, Alex. I read all about Christmas. While I was working, Alex. You fucked her while I was working.

Joel is pulling his jeans on but leaves them unbuttoned since his stomach is still sticky.

I have to go, William. You need to talk to Dimitra about this.

I don't want to, William says softly, nearly whimpering. Alex, please let me talk to you about this. You have to tell me why she would do this.

Alex looks over at Joel. Joel has one sock in his hand and is looking for the other.

All right, William, he says. Let's talk about it.

There's a sound at the other end of the line. Alex, I have to go, says William. I'll call you back.

What was that all about, Joel asks, standing in front of Alex, looking down.

William thinks I slept with Dimitra.

Did you.

Alex doesn't answer.

Joel wipes his stomach off with his hand.
You are a stupid bitch, he says, placing his
sticky hand on Alex's face and shoving him
backward.

- 3 -

D imitra's phone rings and rings and she doesn't answer.

Alex hunts for a shirt that doesn't look dirty. He finds Joel's sock. He is about to put the phone down when Dimitra answers.

William just called me.

Gods.

Yeah, and he said he was going to punch me in the face the next time he sees me and also he wants to rip my balls off.

She is silent. He knows she is putting a cigarette in her mouth and lighting it. He hears her exhale.

Or something like that.

What did you tell him.

He started crying. He wants to talk about it.

Alex, you can't tell him anything.

I know. Dimitra, why does William think

we slept together.

I wrote about Christmas in my journal.

Alex listens to her smoking. He has to save
his cigarettes until he has more money. He
looks in the ashtray for the cigarette Joel
was smoking last night. Joel never smokes
his cigarettes all the way down.

What did you say about Christmas.

Dimitra is silent.

I had my underpants on the whole time, says
Alex, feeling like he is talking to himself.
Does that count as fucking.

You were on top of me, Dimitra says loudly.
You came. I think it qualifies.

There was someone else in the bed with us
that we both actually did fuck.

Technicalities.

I'm sure that made for interesting reading.

I might have skipped a few things.

I'm going to have breakfast with your
boyfriend, says Alex, checking the clock. If
he's still your boyfriend.

I think so, says Dimitra. He left enough coffee
in the pot for me to drink when he went out

this morning.

Why am I supposed to not tell him anything.

Because he'll break up with me if he thinks
I love you.

Everybody knows you love me, says Alex,
rubbing the dry spots on his chin and cheek
that Joel pressed his hand against, trying to
clean it off without having to take a shower.

It's not that, says Dimitra. If he thinks it's
you that I was with, he won't figure out that
me and Joachim are still together.

You're still sleeping with Joachim.

Sometimes. A lot of times. I don't know.

Alex feels cold on his skin.

I am pretty sure he's more straight than gay,
Alex.

I have to go.

Alex, please. If William thinks we slept
together then he won't think—

I have to go, Dimitra. I'll call you later.

– 4 –

Since he is not sure if William will pay for breakfast, Alex orders oatmeal and a glass of water from the tap.

William comes in just after he orders. He's shaved. Alex thinks William is actually a little handsome. Also it seems like he's been crying. He sits down.

Did you read the whole journal, Alex asks first.

No. I wasn't going to read it at all in the first place.

You shouldn't have.

I was cleaning up her desk and I just flipped through it, I don't know why. I saw your name.

You shouldn't have read it, Alex says again.

William bites his lips shut. The waitress comes over.

Are you paying, Alex asks.

William opens his mouth, then closes it and nods.

Can I also have a cup of coffee and change my order please to two eggs over-easy with bacon and toast. He'll have two poached eggs, no bacon. And a small orange juice.

When the waitress leaves William begins crying.

Shit, says Alex.

You know me well enough to order my breakfast, says William.

I was going to order you waffles but I think you need protein.

I don't have any friends except Dimitra's, William says. I moved to this town when she got into school. What am I supposed to do here. I'm buying breakfast for the asshole who slept with my girlfriend. Can you explain to me why that is.

You want to know why she did it.

That's a start.

You should have finished reading the journal.

You told me I shouldn't have read it.

I told you that you shouldn't have read it at all in the first place. But you did. So you should have finished the whole thing.

Do you really think so.

Yes, probably. But if Dimitra is anything like
me then she lies in her journal.

Why would you lie in your journal.

In case the person you live with reads it.

So you didn't sleep with her.

It depends on how you define it.

William can't say anything and then Alex's
coffee comes.

Alex busies himself with stirring sugar and
then cream into the coffee. Because Alex is
skinny like a bird and William has big arms,
Alex decides that if William did punch him
it would really hurt.

William is crying again so Alex gets brave.

Are you going to break up with her.

No. I don't think so.

Are you going to beat me up.

No, Alex.

William has green eyes, almost yellow.
Actually William is very handsome, thinks

34

Alex. At least when he's crying. William is handsome when he is sad and Joel is handsome when he is angry. What does that say about me, Alex asks himself. What does it say about me that I want to kiss William's sad mouth.

Dimitra and I broke up for a very specific reason, says Alex.

She said you wouldn't or couldn't have sex with her.

That's the reason.

So then you wait until after to do it. Alex, it's fucked up.

We didn't plan it at all, William. We did it because suddenly we could. I mean, I wanted to. I wanted to after all this time, finally, and we just got carried away.

Don't tell me.

What I won't tell you, Alex thinks to himself, is that sleeping with Dimitra is a way of sleeping with you.

The waitress comes with their plates. Alex takes his toast and starts eating. He is trying not to look at William's face and looks instead at his eggs.

I'm just supposed to forget about all of this, William says more to himself than Alex. If I want to keep her, I'm supposed to think it doesn't matter.

It doesn't, says Alex, chewing on his toast.
You have her. She wants you. To be with
you. What is the problem.

I can't eat, says William taking the bill. See
you later, Alex.

Alex watches William walk to the cashier.
The waitress comes over.

Should I clear his plate.

No, leave it.

- 5 -

It's completely typical, says Dimitra.

Alex is looking out the window down the street.

What's typical.

He dragged you all the way down there, completely dramatic and then he won't even talk to you.

Why did you write about it in your journal.

Dimitra opens the fridge. Do you want any iced tea.

I haven't talked to Joel about it since he left.

She pours a glass then folds the aluminum foil back over the mouth of the jug.

It's bad for you. Causes cancer.

I lost the lid. She pulls a thin loose cigarette from her pocket, straightens it out.

Do you have another one. I meant the saccharine in the tea not the aluminum.

She takes a knife and cuts an inch and a half
of the cigarette off and hands him the filter
with an inch of cigarette on it.

Joel won't care, she says. She presses her
lips together to dry them and then holds
the filterless bit gently against her mouth
to light it.

He seemed really upset when he left the
diner.

Yeah. But then he came home and made
coffee. The special way he makes it when
he breaks a tea bag over the grounds before
he starts the pot.

Joel didn't even stay over. Just left.

He'll come back.

Do you have any pot.

What am I going to say to him tonight when
he actually wants to talk.

Maybe he won't want to talk.

William will want to talk about all the
reasons I have fidelity issues.

I don't love you, Alex says.

I know.

I love Joachim.

And you can't have him.

Alex puts his hand on Dimitra's throat.
Pushes her against the doorframe. She does
not resist him.

Neither can you.

She looks at him. He leans forward and smells
her neck. Licks her neck and ear.

You taste like him.

- 6 -

It's five in the afternoon and he hasn't done anything all day long besides talk to Dimitra and do a crossword puzzle in the paper at the coffee shop.

Since he didn't have enough money for lunch and is afraid to ask Joel, he takes a long walk through Delaware Park to distract himself from hunger.

He walks along the curb of the perimeter road, glancing into each car window as he passes. He likes his hair longer, growing in snaky curls.

On the front seat of a brown car with a university sticker in the back window, there's a shoulder bag with a knit strap.

Alex walks over to a flower bed and takes a fist-sized rock with smooth edges from the border.

He takes a quick look left and right, and then lobs the rock with a smooth underhand towards the car window.

And keeps walking.

He hears the soft shattering of the window,
sort of like a screen door slamming, but with
a crumbling sound. And still keeps walking.

After about fifty feet, he cross the street and
loops back, passing the car on the other side
of the street, walking another fifty feet past
it.

No one shows up so he crosses the street,
walking along the line of cars, once more
gazing at his reflection in each window. When
he passes the car with the broken window,
he reaches in quickly, sweeps a couple of
the shard-stones from the back and lifts the
bag from the car without slowing his walk.

He waits until he's out of the park on the
Park Street side to look in the bag.

There's a spiral notebook filled with writing,
a small book and an old-fashioned tape
recorder.

Fuck, says Alex, swinging the tape recorder
around and chucking it to the ground. It
busts open and a cassette pops out onto the
ground.

Alex stuffs the notebook and the book back
into the bag and throws it onto the ground
next to the tape recorder.

Let's see what you listen to, asshole, he says,
and grabs the tape on the ground, slides it
into his pocket.

- 7 -

Joel don't work here anymore, the man says.

Right. Joel stopped working at the flower shop because he's working the reception desk at the yoga studio.

Or was that last month.

Alex remembers it's the bookstore Joel is working at now.

Alex, what.

I want to talk to you.

Not a good time. Joel is carrying boxes inside the back entrance of the shop. Alex leans against the brick wall. The sun crashes down, freezes into yellow splinters before it hits the ground.

Alleys are what Alex thinks of as cities.

Are you coming over tonight.

I can't decide.

When.

After midnight. I'm going to Sonny's place first.

Alex feels a spike of jealousy.

What the hell.

Joel stops unpacking. Comes over and stands right in front of Alex.

Do you want to start.

I just want to talk to you, Joel.

Do you. Joel pokes Alex in the chest. Hard. Do you want to tell me I can't hang out with Sonny.

Alex clenches his fist to stop himself from putting his hands up to block Joel's stabbing finger.

Don't you want to know what William wanted to tell me.

Joel steps back and fishes in his pocket for a cigarette. Well he didn't hit you, he says, because you don't have a black eye.

He just wanted to talk about it. He wanted to know why Dimitra did it.

Not why you did it.

Everyone knows why I did it. Don't you.

Joel lights his cigarette and rubs his neck,
looking away. Then he turns back and grabs
Alex by the hair on the back of his head.
Pushes him again the wall. Again Alex
clenches his fists to stop himself from pushing
Joel away.

Joel wraps his arm around Alex's neck and
presses his mouth hard against Alex's face.

Why do you fuck with me, he hisses, his
breath thick with cigarette taste hot on Alex's
skin.

Joel, says Alex, bringing his hands up to hold
Joel's head.

You're mine, Alex, Joel says squeezing Alex
so hard he can't breathe. You're not Dimitra's.
You're not Joachim's. You're not anybody's.
You're mine. Why do you fuck with me.

Alex turns his head to the side and presses
his lips against Joel's neck, the acid of Joel's
cologne numbing his lips. He loses himself in
the crushing feeling, rides the breathlessness.

You think I don't know what you like.

Alex goes limp a little, lets Joel squeeze the
breath out of him.

I'm going to smack the shit of Joachim the
next time I see him.

Joel, don't.

Joel grabs a fistful of Alex's hair and yanks it back so he can look into his eyes. With his other hand he grips Alex's face and forces his mouth open.

Still holding Alex's hair with one hand and his other hand around Alex's chin and mouth, he kisses him hard, thrusts his tongue into Alex's mouth. Alex opens his mouth as wide as he can, leans back in Joel's grip, fumbles for Joel's crotch.

As soon as his fingers brush it, Joel releases him and pushes him away.

I have to work. Get out of here. I'll see you later.

Joel.

Now, Alex. Get going.

Alex wants to ask if he is still going to Sonny's but doesn't. He's burning all over his body, everywhere Joel touched him.

Do you have any pot left, he asks instead.

Joel pulls a rolled-up packet of loose tobacco out of his back pocket. It's inside, he says, tossing it to Alex.

You better be home at midnight, he says, going back into the store. Don't be late, Alex, he

says over his shoulder. I'm going to call home
and you better be there to pick up the phone.

- 8 -

Alex walks down to the corner of Elmwood and North to the building Sonny lives in. His arms, his neck stinging with the marks of Joel's fingers. He sits down on the stoop and takes out the tobacco bag.

He opens the bag and puts a thin line of tobacco into the rolling paper and then drops in several hard clumps of pot, rolling them between his finger tips to loosen them.

He sees Sonny, a block and a half away, skinny and dark, his big head bobbing as he struggles to balance grocery bags.

Who is Sonny cooking dinner for, he thinks, licking the strip and sealing the cigarette. For my boyfriend. Fucking little bitch.

Sonny has to put the bags down, flex his fingers and pick the bags back up.

Alex lights the cigarette and inhales. Has to be careful not to hold the smoke in for very long in case the cop at the corner is watching him.

Sonny is crossing the street.

Hi Alex.

Hi Sonny. Alex leans back on his elbows,
stretches one leg out in front of him. Do
you want a drag.

Sonny sits down in the step beneath Alex.

Heard you had an interesting night.

You talked to Joel.

Yeah.

Alex waits for Sonny to say that Joel is
coming over but he doesn't say.

So. Little Sanjay. What are you up to later.
Going out on the town.

Probably later. Joel's coming over first.

So he said it, thinks Alex, changing his mind
a little bit about Sonny. Not such a little
pussy after all.

What are you and Joel up to, Alex asks,
smoking the joint fully now, drawing slowly,
holding the smoke in.

I'm going to make dinner, says Sonny.

Alex blows the smoke out in a slow stream.

Sonny looks at him with a sad face. Sorry, Alex. Really.

Why, says Alex, standing up. Standing up. Trying to act like Joel. Maybe he should smack Sonny. What the fuck do you mean, Sonny. Why are you sorry. What did you do.

Sonny scrambles up to his feet, fusses with picking up the bags. Funny Sonny. Skinny little Sonny can't even pick up his grocery bags.

I'm talking to you, Alex says, grabbing his arm.

Come inside, says Sonny. Let's talk inside. Not on the street. Alex lets him go. Sonny walks in, leaving the door open behind him.

Alex hears him drop his keys onto the counter. There's a crinkling of plastic as he starts unpacking the groceries.

Alex wants Joachim. Sonny wants Joel. Alex wants Joel. William wants Dimitra. Alex wants William. Dimitra wants Joachim and Joachim wants nothing.

You can stay for dinner if you want to. Really.

I don't think so, Alex calls back. I don't think Joel wants to talk yet.

He goes into the living room. There's a half-

smoked cigarette stubbed out in the ashtray
which he grabs plus a pile of change on the
coffee table which he also grabs.

Joel was pissed and he said didn't want to go
back to your place.

And what did you tell him.

I told him you were a selfish prick, says
Sonny, coming into the living room with a
green pepper and a knife.

Alex laughs. Sanjay for the win.

What the fuck are you making.

Indian food. Are you sure you don't want
to stay.

No man, I don't want to. Alex stands right
next to Sonny, tries to look at him without
losing his cool.

It probably isn't working because Sonny is
sweating but isn't backing up or looking
away. On the other hand he does have a knife
in his hand.

Sonny, listen. Take care of Joel.

Sure.

Listen, Sonny.

What.

I need twenty bucks. I'll pay you back.

Sure, Alex. He goes back into the kitchen.
Comes out with two twenties.

Alex takes the bills. Puts his hand on Sonny's
neck. Sonny's skinny neck. He squeezes it a
little bit. Sonny grimaces but doesn't move.
Keeps looking right at Alex. Swallows. What
would it be like to kiss Sonny, Alex wonders.
Sonny doesn't move.

Alex puts his mouth on him. Sonny's lips are
loose but he does not open them. Alex licks
Sonny's lips with his tongue. Sonny does not
tense. He does not move.

Good kid, says Alex, letting go and stuffing
the bills in his pocket.

See you, he calls out as he runs down the
stairs, leaving the door open behind him.

- 9 -

It's weird, says Dimitra. I don't want to
lose him.

She is lying between Joachim's legs, her cheek
resting on his thigh. He is lying back on the
pillows, his head leaning back so he can look
out the window at the gray sky, blow smoke
out the window.

Alex or William.

Either, I suppose.

You don't want to have me instead, Joachim
asks her, smiling. He knows the answer.

She turns her face to kiss his leg just below
the band of his underpants. She pulls his leg
a little higher so the bare skin of his thigh
rests on her collarbone.

I wouldn't do your dishes, says Joachim, or
make coffee for you when you come home
from work.

He doesn't even know I don't like coffee,
she says.

He is your little bitch, he agrees. And you are a little heartless. But I like a guy who can make a pot of coffee like that.

He has a secret, she says, closing her eyes to the bright light coming in through the window.

What's the secret.

I can't tell you. You'll think it's gross.

Joachim smiles.

Do you really think I'm heartless, she asks, shifting herself up, pushing his legs apart so she can pillow her cheek on his crotch. She places his left hand on her head. Now she can lie down, see his chin, speckled with stubbles, doesn't have to look at his eyes.

He's rooting around on the night table for something. His watch. He's checking the time.

You don't have to leave. William is working at the bar and he's going to be out until way way late. Four o'clock probably.

Do you love Alex she wants to know and Joachim doesn't answer.

What's heartless about you, he says. You love William. You'll never leave him. He thinks you are the little wife and this—

This I'm tired of already, she says.

Already, he asks.

He watches the candle burning, the same candle for the last several weeks. He wants it to burn out finally.

What is the secret.

Do you love Alex, she asks.

Tell me the secret.

Ugh, she says, closing her eyes. It's tea. He breaks a bag of tea and sprinkles it over the coffee.

Every time he comes to the apartment he lights the candle, wanting to finish it. And when he finishes the candle, he wants to be finished with Dimitra.

Do you love Alex, she asks again.

I want to, he says. What are you tired of.

Not tired of you. Tired of. What. This feeling. Or being bored with someone I love. And then being bored by cheating.

It's not what you think is going to happen, he agrees, putting out his cigarette.

- 10 -

Alex walks back through the park. There's a man at the car with the broken window. He is trying to sweep pebbles of glass from the car seat out onto the grass.

Bad luck, says Alex.

The man straightens. He's bigger than Alex. Not difficult to be. Taller too. Dark-skinned, clean cut. Cute.

What is it, Alex thinks, looking at the man's broad shoulders. Why am I so fucking skinny. Should I start eating meat again.

Yeah, the man says. They took some stuff.

Sometimes if you look around, you find something. That happened to me once. I'll help you look.

Sure, he says. Thanks. I'm Arjun.

Alex.

He walks alongside Arjun in the twilight, trying to catch a look of him in the corner of his eye. Arjun stops every once in a while to look around. Alex slows down too.

What did you lose, he asks.

A tape recorder from school.

You go to college.

I'm a medical student.

What's on the tape.

The other man laughs.

He's beautiful, thinks Alex. Is it weird that I
have never hooked up with an Indian guy. Is
that why I don't like Sonny, he wonders then.
No, I don't like Sonny because he's a girl.

The tape, Arjun says, is my Latin homework.

I have to change my mind about you, says
Alex.

Why.

Because you're a Latin-loving queer, Alex
says and laughs. And then gets ready to run
if he has too.

Arjun yanks him close. I don't like that word,
he says.

It hurts. Let go. I was kidding. I'm gay too.

Arjun drops Alex's arm.

I'll give you a twenty if you help me find my bag.

I got some time, says Alex.

They walk across the park towards Park Street. Alex leads him on. Then when they are close to the place he says, Is this your bag.

Look at that, says Arjun, picking up the bag. They didn't take my notebook or my book.

And is this yours, Alex picks up the tape recorder.

Arjun takes it and puts it into the bag.

Alex puts his hand in his pocket, feels the plastic cassette. Can't put it back now.

I live over there.

They walk across the street to a blue row house. Arjun unlocks the door and they go upstairs.

While he is in the kitchen, pouring something, Alex stands in the living room, his hand in his pocket around the cassette. Where's my twenty bucks, he yells.

Arjun comes back into the room, two glasses in his hand. I'll give you twenty more if you hang out for a little bit.

What do you want me to do.

Just. Just do what I tell you to do. And then next time do it without me telling you. Hit me.

What.

Not with your fist. Slap me. On the face. Not near my eye. On my cheek. But hard.

Alex feels Joel's hand on his face that morning.

Arjun is looking at him. Waiting.

Alex slaps his cheek. His hand burns. That hard enough.

You can punch me if you want. In the stomach. Really punch me but not superhard. Do you know how to punch.

Alex has never punched anyone but he has been punched. Yeah, I know how to do it, he says.

You can really punch me. I'm asking you to. Not really hard but a little bit. But tell me first before you do it.

Alex thinks about Joel. He makes his little hand into a fist. Sometimes when Joel is really rough with him, he likes it. Maybe this is like that. He wants to be punched.

Are you ready.

Yes.

He punches him in the stomach. Hard.

Arjun sags as the air is knocked out of him.
He grabs on to Alex. His mouth on Alex's
shirt.

That what you wanted.

Yes. Now put your hand on my throat.
Now choke me. Just a little. Not really. But
squeeze.

Alex is holding Arjun's throat. I can't. I don't
want to.

Put your forearm on my throat. And then
just press a little. Just a little.

So this is the thing you like. Why.

I don't know. Do you like doing it.

Yeah, kind of.

And you never have before.

Not exactly. What else do you want me to
do to you.

Anything. Anything you want.

Alex thinks about Joachim, his little red
mouth. How soft his skin is. His strange
yellow eyes. He thinks of the warmth in
Arjun's breath, how he is waiting for Alex
to hurt him.

And then hurt him again some more.

He is thinking about Joel's hands on him. Roughly. Sometimes while kissing. And sometimes not.

Alex goes over to the stereo and takes the cassette out of his pocket.

Hey, says Arjun in surprise.

Alex slides the tape into the stereo. Presses play.

Arjun's voice reciting Latin comes out of the speakers.

What the fuck is this. What did you do.

All right, says Alex, very tired. Where's my money.

SEWN

Shorn. I came into the world emerging. Sound of the waves thundering.

Twenty-six. With blue-black hair. Dark skin. & purple eyes. And where are my missing twenty-five years.

I know. But can't tell.

I have a curse of silence that has sewn my mouth shut.

On the beach I find a piece of driftwood, knotted like a witch's finger, bleached white and smooth as bone by eons of the ocean's trembling.

Which loops back on itself. *(My nails break on the rocks.)*

(My mouth bleeds.)

I weigh my choices:

1) Let the space remain open & have a magic mirror:

> *In a town I remember, a woman beats the*
> *dark cotton against the rocks at the river.*
>
> *In the town which doesn't exist yet, a woman who*
> *hasn't been born opens the curtains to sun.*

Or:

2) Thread it carefully with silk. No better yet: fishing twine. A tapestry: what I've seen in the craft stores called a dream-net. A tapestry of memories. Its purpose is to catch dreams.

An unlikely solution to my searing & strange obsession. An obsession which   like my others   has roots in logic but routes of fulfillment in magic.

Am I remembering a past life or dreaming up lives that haven't happened yet?

The sun. Sonorous.

Waves of dolor.

The mountains fading stained by spilt tea: the ocean is a dangerous place.

In the town I remember a woman.

There is an ache in my neck.

& I. & I. I.

Beaten to listlessness by the thundering waves.

Black face of the moon sliding out of the sun.

My heart's tight knot would unravel & my mystery would unfog.

I do not want my heart to unravel. I will save the thread with which I would have sewn the net. And who can tell if such an object fulfills its purpose?

The driftwood I'll use not as a frame to catch the past but as a portal through which to gaze at what is coming.

So I return home. *How do I know which cabin is mine?* & do the spell for far-seeing.

Holding an unwashed spud loosely between your palms, envision your beloved's face strongly.

Vigorously shake/rub the potato between the palms. Place the potato in a quart of fresh, cold water: a transparent container, preferably glass.

Chant a mantra. Once the potato begins sprouting, throw the potato away. Keep the water. You will be able to see the face of your beloved in the water.

Do not cook the potato, dangerous cannibal.

Throw the potato away. Throw it away.

Important: a spell set on someone comes back on its caster three times.

A love spell sent will induce love in the maker. & a curse will return with its wrath.

You could not send a curse to me.

In an effort—

       for example—

              to silence me.

It would roll off my back.

I think.

I watch the phases of the moon carefully.

I'm told my strength comes with the old moon waning into the new moon: the strength of ending. In order to have new life.

The farmer slashes the forest & then burns the stumps to the ground.

My tragic role: I am that which destroys for new growth.

Someone who is habitually sweeping things away.
& I watch them go.

My empty hands clenching & unclenching.

My friend comes to show me how to set up my altar. In fours:

Air: a small, limp balloon from someone's wedding.

Water: a shallow bowl, wooden, filled.

Fire: incense cones, vanilla.

Earth: clay molded in the shape of a crescent moon. For her power: the waxing moon. Bringing things to their fruition.

Her athame: not a knife but a wooden cooking spoon. She says she does not have to show her steel. The cooking spoon is better than a magic wand, she says. Look at the magic that comes from it already: spaghetti sauce, chicken curry, chocolate fondue.

She knows her spices: which powders, roots, tinctures, to drop into the pot. & stirs. Beckoning to beguile.

She bewitched me with a feast: spinach salad, mandarin oranges with walnuts. Chicken biryani. Strawberries & chocolate fondue.

But she has plain spinach. A peeled mandarin orange. No walnuts. Plain rice. & strawberries without chocolate. & I say: you have your own curse, you who nurture things to their fruition cannot but lose them.

She says: it is the curse of being a mother. & I think

> *no it is that of the ocean, pounding and pounding.*
> *My feet are pounding on the rocks. My feet are shattering to*
> *splinters—*

> *I remember: nothing*

> *I came into the world emerging. Twenty-six.*
> *With blue-black hair. Dark skin.*

> *& purple eyes.*
> *& I have told no one*

> *I have a curse of silence that has sewn*

> *my mouth*

> *shut.*

The recipe she won't teach me, the one I really want, I have to track down on my own, combing through used bookstores and antique places in every town I visit. I find it in an old town in the Hudson Valley, one founded in 1692.

Recipe: Kali's blood potion.

Origin: Kali-Ma. Third face. Destroyer. Mother who devours her own children.

> Monsoons. Rain & thunder & lightning. Plagues. Cyclones. Earthquakes. Et cetera.

Indications:

To eat your own creation. To vomit from yourself the fruits of your labor. To rid yourself of good intentions misshapen. To remember something deep buried.

Ingredients:

> Soured milk.
> Grease drippings from twice-boiled meat.
> Apple cores.
> Pennyroyal.
> Saliva.
> Nut shells.
> Hair clippings.
> Finger nails.
> Beetroot.

Blend well. Serve hot. With a wilted daisy for garnish.

You will forget. Whatever it is you want to forget. You will forget that you have forgotten.

*

Head cradled in my hands. A citronella candle, a blanket: of stars in the sky.

Points: like on the skin of a dark red apple. Four stories up makes the horizon like water.

Church steeples, trees. At the edge of a tea cup. A city's rage congeals on the streets, grease & grime. Muck.

    Congeals into dirt on the windows & dust on the statues. & rises into fog. & those who lie on rooftops

hiding amongst weathervanes,
Antennae, chimneys,
Roosting with the pigeons

     Can feel it collecting on their skin. Dewy. Sticky. The rage of a city rising into night.

Years since I can sleep soundly on the ground.

I come up instead to the sky. Where sometimes I feel like part of my spirit—lost like a bird—might find me waiting, a migratory destination.

Boneless, my dream:

Running amongst rocks. A dream of pursuit.

I am not (*my nails shatter on the rocks*) being chased.

I am running after someone.   Who is burning.

   (did I set this fire?)

I know this place. *(I set this fire)*. No. I do not know this place because I do not know that person who is running away. On fire. & I :

Running.

Over the rocks.   My fingernails are breaking.

Splitting apart.   *(shattering—)*

I only know one alphabet, the plain one, the one of spoken words.

Odin hung at the tree of knowledge for eight days. He shook with pain & the branches of the tree snapped & fell.

When he loosened the noose & came down from the tree, the branches had fallen into a pattern: an alphabet. The runes. They were a secret alphabet which spelled the untold words.

They unraveled mountains & raised tsunami from rocks.

I went to hang from the tree of knowledge whose roots reach down into the earth to feed in the land of death *(there is a smell of burning hair)* & the land of fire.

I went to find myself runes: it is no small thing *(I dream of myself twice)* to try & hang oneself.

> I woke when twenty-six days had passed. One day for each year of my young   & unremembered   life.

> Two rune alphabets had fallen & were hopelessly mixed together. Jumbled.

The words they might have spelled were shattered ciphers.

But weirdly, I remember this: binding spell:

To silence someone. To prevent a secret from being told or a face from being revealed.

Necessary: strong thread.

Even better: fishing twine.

A sharp needle.
                            (a tanner's needle and fishing twine)

A button.

Any article of clothing you might commonly wear.

Position the button in an inconspicuous place, for example, inside a pocket, under the hem. With a desire for silence burning in your heart & lips clamped firmly between the teeth, stitch the button to the fabric with swift & determined strokes: with the secret bound. Fettered: not to be released until the button falls from the fabric.

Infuse your enforcement of silence into the thread with the sympathy of the damned.

I am always putting myself into things. My fingers are always getting caught in zippers. Bumping into tables. I shouldn't be able to be in two places at once, but I've somehow stumbled onto the ability.

> In my dreams perhaps, dredging up the submerged
> memory of being able to walk through walls, walk on
> water, to soothe ashes back into a burned woman, to
> crush diamonds back to coal, with a wayward phrase send
> a man crawling backwards on his fins into the ocean.

There was a time when I would pick up a goblet to toast & my fingers would turn to crystal. If I sat down in a chair my legs might turn to wood. Walking in a street was a potential disaster: it might give me feet of stone.

Close the shutters, I may turn into wind—

Extinguish all the lamps, I am becoming light—

I am still unsure of myself. Frightened to eat some days for fear of dissolving. On bad days even afraid to breathe: I might exhale my spirit right out of my body & unable to return be borne aloft into the clouds.

What a plain history could have been written. Walking on floorboards. Or slipping between them. Into the earth. Into the sewers. Rushing south with the waters.

Following the migration patterns of the birds, flying unseen thousands of feet above.

I went to a party once where someone asked me what I thought about dreams & magic. & I said:

I do not yet know my own heart.

What I thought but did not say:

The moon. The pulling of the tides. The earth's turning. Waking. Sleeping. Dreaming. *Waking.*

& I stopped listening to the talk about magic & looked at the tulip on the table. If I had come a week earlier it would only have been a bulb. Had I come a week later it would have wilted.

On the roof I understood.

The precipice. Heart, I can feel myself falling. Dizzy like a bird.

> I remember being told that divers who go
> into the depths of the ocean do not wish to
> return. Surrounded by expanse. Movement is
> slowed. Sound amplified. Every small motion
> is an experience. Sight is dimmed. & fish
> swim up against them. & they are pulled into
> the center of the life of the ocean. & their
> hearts fly open like birds. & they cannot
> think to swim to the surface. The thought
> of emerging is so painful to them that they
> stay in the deep. & drown.

& when one does return the thought of the ocean is overpowering, its fluidity & grace will always draw the diver back into the depths.

I was at the edge of the roof for hours. Finally pushing myself away on numb arms. My head was singing empty. My eyes had widened to cover my face. I had risen into the gables   the arches above the city   with the gargoyles & rain clouds.

What did I hope to gain by *(I was named then for speaking—)* forsaking the loom & keeping my driftwood whole?

What do I need with more dreams? I would *(dissipate into smoke)* weave over the hole at this minute, cover up the whole & use that looped driftwood at last as a dream net—this minute—had I not used the only fishing twine in the house for the binding spell.

Strange compulsion. The same compulsion that has sewn my mouth shut.

So the fishing twine is gone. The dream net unmade. & me: silent. Halfway to the horizon. My dreams: elusive.

We are trained with the desire to secrecy.

71

Childhood diaries with metal locks.

Those secrets which could never be told are being carried in the wind, rising on storm clouds, combing the surface of our skin dark & tormented. Until

they come to rest in the eye of the hurricane: haunted: still: dangerous.

Every child who received a diary with a lock also received a key. A key identical to any other diary key. The dream of security.

Manufactured in smoke & dissipated in the same breath which sighed: my secrets are safe now.

I am certain that the secrets of my dreams which were locked away by someone or something could be opened by an identical key. I am certain I do not have to trace my muteness to its source in order to begin unraveling. Yet.

But I have a secret I *can* tell you. Spell for privacy:

You are joined with this book.

If you hold it you will come away with papercuts under your fingernails.

Your eyes will grow wide into I.

Your ears will close tight as M.

Your skin will become like paper. You will cry tears of india ink.

★

I was seven when I first heard words. For six years it had been silence. & darkness. I knew only one word—not "water" as you might think, no my long road ended in a different place—"earth." I did not speak for years after that. By the time I was ten I understood the moon & was counting my birthday by its phases.

When I was twelve & standing on top of a barrow I flew for the first time. So easy. I leaned as far forward as I could & put my arms out. I had never seen something fall. & so I didn't fall. I flew. Such an easy thing but so difficult. Try it.

But not from a roof top.

& on my thirteenth birthday dreams began. Of other boys, they looked like me but weren't me. One with bright red hair and skin so pale I could see blue veins beneath the surface, another with a dusky complexion and rich brown eyes. But all with my face. And always as time passed their skin and hair would darken—the face always unchanging, my face staring out at me as if from a mirror.

But I began to believe I myself was the reflection.

On my sixteenth birthday I awoke from a night of fitful dreams—

Of a boy running. With dark skin & bleeding fingers. On the rocks—

two hundred & eight moons since my birth:

With purple eyes.

    & that afternoon I discovered there is a price
    for everything.

Test of earth: packed earth pressing into the back of
          my head, the stone heavy on my chest.
          But my chest did not collapse. My ribs
          would not shatter. My spirit would
          not allow it. My skull was becoming
          clay. My smooth hands grasping the
          rock becoming heavier & heavier, skin
          turning to granite.

73

Test of air: they dragged me up to the roof.

                                & threw me from it. Had I only fallen, broken a few bones, perhaps, who knows what might have happened next, but instead:

                                The wind rushed up to meet me & slowed me to a hover. As I fell down through it I twisted in the air. & landed on all fours.

It did not help my case that there happened to be a black cat lurking in the doorway of the building in front of which I had the misfortune to fall.

Test of water: they strapped me to a wooden chair which hung from a long pole. & lowered me into the lake.

                                Two choices:

                                1) become like the wood & remain imprisoned in the chair until it disintegrated; or

                                2) become like the water & swim free: part of the ocean, but lost to my body forever. I thought too long & they pulled me from the lake. Alive & coughing up peat-flavored water.

The ropes   still wet   were carried to the pole & used to tie me to it.

I knew about the last test. I had heard about it & the details of my last days went flying forth: they did not play themselves out in my head as I had often heard told. They scattered & I forgot everything: who I was. Where I had come from. Why this was happening. As the flames sizzled the wet ropes & the heat rushed inward, I thought: a mercy: I will suffocate before the flames actually burn me. & then I remembered my first word in that life:

> I am Fire. Mine is the power to slash & burn the field like the farmer.

My skin beginning to cook, my throat beginning to close, my hair up in flames, my only thought:

> Oh restless wandering love, how will you come back to yourself? & so, sliding easily out of the ropes & rising up the pole to join the smoke & sparks of fire,

I quietly gave up the ghost.

My only place: a name on a commemorative plaque. For no sin which could be named on it.

A nameless sin of which I was later acquitted   some years later. Over the course of the years I would return over & over to that plaque.

—which I first saw when I woke up under it. In a churchyard I didn't recognize. With no memory of the years that came before. On May 30, 1992—

a strangely inconspicuous visitor to the churchyard   my purple eyes hidden behind dark glasses   hoping to remember.

But my suspicion: the details will not be found on a plaque
                        or in a courtyard but instead:
                        in my dreams.

Which I am   lacking dependable technology   unable to catch.

The oceans of the world each spread out. & each has its own reasons to throw me up   or hold from me   my magical looped driftwood: for my dream-net.

> Atlantic: angry. I walked up & down the shores picking through trash & bottles. Of all things to throw up: not seaweed or clamshells. Waste. After centuries of throwing in: blood   gold   babies.

> Pacific: roaring at me into its vastness. Covering half the whole world. I sometimes pretend I can smell the cooking, the car fumes of Asia carried over the ocean. The fog made mountains into paper & endless & still. Rolling. & rolling. & back & back.

> Indian ocean: giving salt: which preserves meat. Which destroys plants. Bringing water: which nourishes. & drowns. Bringing monsoons. & I think: this is the ocean that will bring me up my looped driftwood. These are the beaches on which my staunch & fleeing soul might finally come to rest, knotted up in driftwood.

Perfectly smooth, widely looped. Somewhere in the twelve-foot waves. Is my driftwood.

Somewhere among the camel rides & discarded peach pits. Is my driftwood.

Spirited away to a street-side bazaar. I wandered the streets of the now no longer named   Madras   in search of it.

Now that someone else has lifted it from the ocean with his own intentions will it be contaminated with their dreams? Will I be able to sort mine from theirs?

Or do we all dream the same dream each night?

And some of us just remember certain parts better than others?

> *Or will it be the way it was with the mixed-up alphabets? I*
> *am looking for the driftwood in Chennai, but it waits for me*
> *in Madras...*

If I only had the ability of the old Hindu goddesses and gods   to
be in two places at once   there would be no need to go back to that
church all the time   in my inconspicuous disguise. I could leave
myself   & my memories   burning there & go about my business.

(Which is currently: deciphering my dreams & untangling the
past—)

There would be no reason to go & read those names. & their
absolution.

Sometimes in my sleep, in my dreams I rise up clear out of my body
& rush through the window into the air. Drawn like a magnet to
the churchyard. I remember feeling like that once before. When I
slid up the stake & scattered my spirit to the four winds.

Now I am terrified of sleeping. Terrified I will rise up out of my
body responding to the peculiarities of my   now unremembered
dreams. & pushing & straining on that silver cord   which over
the years has become tangled & knotted with use   & fly up above
my body like a kite. Now I go into the bed with small weights
fastened to my ankles.

On my twelfth birthday I began to speak. & never stopped.

Harsh words. In grating tones. Incendiary   ironically. I had been
silent for twelve years. & needed to make up for that lost time. & so
I spoke in an unnatural voice. Unpracticed. Unmeasured. Strident.
A greeting sounded like a growling curse, a refusal   a rebuke.

& no words fit what my heart felt.

77

I perceived only the silence. & my words filling it. My prescience into the past sent warnings in all directions. That if I continued speaking: I would never be able to stop. That speaking was an affliction. That the maxim: children should be seen & not heard: did nothing for my cause.

When   on my sixteenth birthday   like a charm from a first life my light skin began to darken & my red hair turned brown and then black and then nearly blue-black & my eyes began to streak into purple, what might have been precocious or obnoxious became dangerous. & blasphemous.

There was a forest near that town. What was then wilderness is now an exit loop on the turnpike. People told lurid stories: women dancing for beasts. I went to the forest often. & spoke of it with many people. In my stilted   harsh   voice. & when the others were named, I was named.

My mouth wide open: lurid things coming out. Rusty, remembered curses.

Twenty-six. Only ten of those years hearing voices. It always happens like this. But I will not burn. My body will not become ash. My spirit will escape up the stake.

★

Rebecca puts her cooking wand away & shakes the runes for me. I hear them softly knocking together in her black bag.

She puts the bag down: Pull the runes out, she says. My wide hands fit more comfortably around a tarot deck.

My eyes need the depth of color. I am afraid one rune won't be enough. I have lived lives stretching across five hundred years by my count   at least   I need five runes

at least. & each with its symbol. & name:

78

which is not necessarily congruous with its divinatory meaning. They are   like us   complicated. I have made a choice & need to know from her: is it the right one? But this is impossible.

She looks at the rune & tells me: there is a choice. It is a grave one. It will reverberate for the rest of your life. Or longer, she adds.

I remember the choice I made: to fly up from the stake. & outwards to the four winds.

On may 30, 1984 a Tuesday—

          —for Tir, Norse mythos, blind god of justice & war: war & justice being   in their ideal permutation   blind—

—the moon crossed over the sun. But not completely. A slight crescent remained. What scientists call: an annular eclipse.

Although the light of the sun was stilled by the black disk of the moon, the corona, the blinding quality remained. Wind whipped up from nowhere, strong: knocking the plaque from the church wall.

Dogs began barking hideously. The cats simply vanished. Into air. Each color assumed a torrid, florid air. Light green leaves: chartreuse. Pink flowers: magenta. Blue sky: aqua. Like the ocean. & a chill of late October dropped into the churchyard.

& in the   not completely   aligning moment of the sun & moon, the light of the crescent burst out smoke & fire & ashes & skin came racing together from east & west & north & south & I

came into the world.   *Emerging.*

                    A look of thunder in my eyes.
                    Half a curse in my throat. Only
                    slightly surprised to be alive. &
                    sixteen. With purple eyes. My
                    skin burning as if sunburned.

With a stiff & aching neck: as if
it was broken. With absolutely
no memory of my birth.

North wind: skin. The face of things. Demanding & harsh. With
no deception: or charm.

South wind: fire. The heart of things. Guileful. Cunning. Which
throws shadows & sparks. Which swallows whole.

East wind: smoke. The beginning of things. Being borne out of
a cloud of obfuscation. Clarity hazed. The mists.

West wind: ashes. Where things come clean. Penitent. The leftovers.
Which sit in urns. Or is smudged onto the foreheads of the faithful.

I deal my tarot like poker. With each successive hand, the stakes
go higher. There is no bluff to call.

Signifier: two of coins. Someone so innocent there is a deception.
So deceptive there is an innocence. An artist who can go on forever:
who is juggling infinity.

Crossed by: reversed six of cups. The loss of riches. Or   as in
my case   of memory.

Foundation: the high priestess. Wisdom. Understanding. My
mother. The mother.

Past: ace of wands. Primal fire of Prometheus. Or Lucifer   whose
name means: bringer of light. The gift. & the conflagration.

Present: hermit. One   me   gone in search of what he does not
know. Solitude. Bereavement.

Future: death. Metamorphosis. Swift. Sudden. & involuntary.

My effect: six of swords. Science. New things. Magic. Secrets.

My affliction: four of swords. Respite. A lull in the battle.

My fear or my dream: strength. A conquest. A victory.

Outcome: hanged man. Suspension. Uncertain outcome. Lack of resolution.

Of course I think then of the night I

> woke up in the churchyard. I
> went to the rooftop to look
> out at the city, yellow.

After waking from a spiritless birth I wanted to know   badly which house was my home.

But in my deepest heart I knew no home. I knew my body had changed. Or seemed to. My features have remained each time an odd mix of European & Asian. My accent has remained constant, musical: a leprechaun's. My skin darkens to brown: an Arab, an African, an Indian. The vibrant red always burning from my hair, my green eyes always darkened to purple.

> —although apparently the cosmetic & psychic senses of beauty have changed. Purple eyes are no longer the mark of evil but merely a curiosity. Or beauty in & of themselves: the other day I saw a woman in the street with purple eyes which   unlike mine   were not her own, but an affectation. Did I burn so thoroughly for what   a mere few centuries later   would become fashion?—

My eyes help me to see inside my mind & heart. I can focus naturally on a thought & instantly I can see it. In sharp relief. They can see completely around me. I have no peripheral vision. Everything is exactly in front of me. One of my friends asked me: do you have eyes in back of your head? I put my hands back there   groping panicked.

81

Pieces are flying together then.

I was driving my car today   Tuesday, may 30, 1992: eight years
to the day since I awoke in the churchyard, leaning against the
church, my neck at an odd angle:

> Which has resulted in an
> eight-year-long neck ache

> & I leaned forward.

Glanced up. To look at the   yet another annular   eclipse with
my naked eye—

> As I had been warned not
> to do. Over & over.

—for almost ten seconds. The crescent of the sun was
burned onto my eye. I could see it   blue   wherever I looked. I
almost kept looking. & then I panicked with the thought:

> that I had burned all the purple out of my
> eyes. That I wouldn't be able to see any more.

I pulled over on the side of the highway. Ran down the embankment
to a little pond in the field. Looked into the water. Like Narcissus.
Like a painter painting a self-portrait. Perfect yet imperfect. &
looked at the image trying to make sure the purple was still there.
& behind me high in the sky: the crescent of the sun. Looking
like the moon. Who was the boy with the purple eyes who always
came back to claim me?

Because of the moon, because of this half-phase, this sun-like moon,

Me: burning.   Me: drowning.

Me: thrown aloft. Landing on all fours.
Me: bleeding.
Sliding up the burning maypole.

                                      Scattered to the four winds.

(shattered—)

& the crescent sun behind me. Shining through my hair. Making
it look red. For just long enough.

                             My hands to my face. & a remembrance:

This is who I am.
That is who I am.

Standing by the side of the road. The wind whipping up the grass in
ripples. The sky: aqua. The grass: chartreuse. My hands: molasses.
My hair: on fire.

    & the haunted spirit inside me shakes   restless.
    Groans in pain.

With tender & scarred hands, my back arches to the black moon
sliding out of the sun.

                            ★

Another dream.

A boy climbing rocks. Running. A boy

with dark brown skin. Like the color my skin always turns to.

Running away. With blue black hair. Silky. & purple eyes: panicked.
His hands are bleeding. His fingernails split against the rocks.

He appears sometimes as his own dreams: other times he advances
from the smoke, intruding in my other dreams, a ghost demanding
more than his fair share of time.

The next morning I wash & I see his face in the mirror: groggy. There is only one thing for me to do. The only clue I have. The only solid piece in the miasma of visions around me.

So when I once patrolled the streets of   the now no-longer-named Madras for the driftwood to make my dream-net, now I walk up & down the aisles of the supermarket looking for the right bottle: jet-black, no. Natural black, no. Blue-black.

My hair is supposed to be the darkest black. With not a trace of color in it. Whatever first memory possesses me haunts my body in ways I cannot control. Black: absence of death. & life. Devoid.

After lathering the dye   which smells faintly of wine   I wait thirty minutes: fidgeting. Be reasonable, I think:

You've waited five hundred years for this.
Wait a little longer.

& when I washed it out my hair was like black velvet & I looked into the mirror and saw: him. Him in my dreams.

& I remembered: five hundred years, yes: 1492. The boy on the rocks. Bleeding.

& the plaque in the churchyard, reading: 1692. A boy with red hair & green eyes. Burning. Sliding up the stake.

I dream of myself twice.

Rebecca uses her magic wand/cooking spoon to cook me a meal of remembrance.

Cooks: the last legal witches.

Spanish rice.

Ginger coming fresh through Granada in Arab hands on the roads of North Africa.

> Hands which were brutally severed from
> their wrists & arms in 1492.

If I close my eyes & hold my ear to a sea shell I can hear the sound of bones being crushed.

One memory is easy to follow. With two it is almost impossible. Like jumbling two jigsaw puzzles together & trying to solve both into only one picture.

I am afraid that once I put it all together the end result   me   will be a fragmented unrecognizable mess.

> My curse of words: my curse for being
> unable to bear the pain. & passing out:
> hanging too long from the tree of
> knowledge: ending up with too many
> alphabets.

With my new black hair I've opened up a door. Unlocked a mystery. But things have not come together any clearer. I go back   as has become the custom when I am baffled: particularly by dreams which turn into reality but remain unrecognized   to the churchyard.

Where I sit on the steps underneath the plaque with the name which is not my name. When I was acquitted of no sin which could be named.

The tour guide has brought a large group of people around the plaque. Which either does not notice my   other-worldly yet corporeal presence or notices but   with typical New England reserve   is too polite to comment

on a black-haired purple-eyed dark-
skinned vagabond slumped against the
plaque. Somewhat disrupting their view.

& I remember the cooking of my flesh. The burning of my hair.
& the stiffness in my neck when I awoke here. On my sixteenth
birthday. & I hear the sound of crows. Am short of breath. Feel a
chafing on my neck. & the jerk of my throat.

Somewhere in another lifetime I hear the tour
guide saying: *contrary to popular belief there were no
witch burnings here. These witches were all hanged.*

& the shock jerks me right up out of my body. It slumps over onto
the floor. Forgotten for a moment. Another town drunk, & I:

standing on a platform. The air is hot. The rope is thick. Only
seven knots tied in it instead of the full   & standard   eight.
Because I am only a boy: sixteen.

There are bells ringing. Church bells. There is a man in
black whispering words of mercy for my soul. Without thinking
I begin whispering words of mercy for his soul. His eyes widen
in panic & are locked to mine. Which once were a pleasing green
& have now darkened: to purple.

He backs away from me, muttering. & falls off the platform. &
breaks his leg. The other men swear & strike me on the cheek, hard.

I turn unto them the other.

Which they also strike.

& loosen my noose to tie in it the eighth knot. The cries are frantic
around us. One old, old woman muttering a curse. But I think:

God's Mother pray for me: now & the hour of my death.

Which today is the same thing.

& the lever snaps forward & my head snaps up.

& in the instant the neck breaks I am thrown from my body with shattering force.

> *Looking back I see myself hanging.*
> *Not limp: thrashing. My silver cord*
> *is fraying & snapping.*

I fight the mad urge to fly back into the body. Back home.

To die. Instead I lie back on the current of the wind & fall into stupor. Giving up the ghost.

& the burning I don't know. The boy with red hair who burned on the maypole I do not know. His red hair   the hair which burned is the hair I cannot restore. He burned somewhere else. Not at this church. I may need that dream-net after all.

What other violence & mystery will I find? I'm shaking in terror as I sink down wearily into the slumped body on the steps of the church. Which has been prodded by a passing policeman.

When my skin burns it surprises me. When I feel anger. Hot flashes. Or grief.

My fingertips are numb. My neck is sore. I am continually massaging it.

My skin always burns.

Every muscle aches constantly. From the thrashing.

My hair flying up & my eyes bloodshot.

I sag under the weight of my lives.

When my fingernails split climbing the rock. When my head jerked up to the New England sky. When my spirit slid up the stake.

My hair   which I had taken to shaving   always grew back to full length by the next old moon.

When companies began marketing colored contact lenses I rejoiced. & bought them by the bucketful. But my eyes burned through them in days.

Already I can see the velvet black of this dye browning at its ends. Soon I will have spotted leopard hair.

If I seem obsessed by the cosmetics of my fate it is only because somehow I know: the appearance & surface are linked to what churns underneath.

A problem which must be untangled. A knot which must be untied. Like the last knot in my noose. & I panic, remembering Alexander who was called: Great   & the prophecy of the Gordian knot. That whoever untied the knot would rule. He slashed through the knot & severed the rope. Sealing his own fate. Inscribing his own death.

I fiddle with my shoelaces trying to teach myself how to untie without cutting.

In the book I am reading, ships trawl a lake where a body has drowned. They fire cannons over the water. Hoping that the shock & sound will cause the submerged body to rise. Failing that they comb the shores with nets. Hoping to raise something. They catch stones & seaweed & fish. & sometimes the submerged body will emerge. & sometimes it never does.

& years later   theoretically   it washes ashore miles from where it first descended into the deep. That is how my spirit is: a body which has drowned. Vanished. & I trawl for it using snatches of memory. Spells & incantations. To try to find my lonely wandering spirit: that ghost I gave up.

What drowned bodies   & evidently my spirit   don't learn: a body will not submerge unless it swallows water or is caught by something. The natural state of the body is: to float on water.

Similarly: if one goes out of one's body, eyes rolled back to the sky: the ghost will float up. & out. To the four winds.

There are three fates. In some mythologies they are mentioned by names. In others they do not exist as entities but as aspects of life.

First fate: sits weaving life into thread. She is the creator.

Third fate: is the one wielding the scissors. Who cuts the Thread. She is the destroyer.

They are the legendary ones. Goddesses. But the small sister between them:

Second fate: with her small hands   & large fingers   she measures a billion or more threads at once. & never tangles a single one.

I picture my thread in her fingers. Are there two? Three? More? Each thread between each finger being measured at once? Or does she measure the new one only after the old one has been cut?

Or perhaps it is all one thread, old & knotted. Each death represented by a knot in the thread: which would explain my preoccupation with knots.

Am I being woven two at a time? Is that where my dreams are coming from? & the boy with red hair who was burned? Is that me? & the boy with black hair climbing the rocks? Are they both me? Or neither?

Now that the eclipse has burned the purple from my eyes I worry & fret that I will see the truth when it finally comes in front of me. It is better to worry about that than worry that the truth will never come at all. Or that there is no truth.

My eyes brought me grief when they caused me to be named in 1691. & when I was asked my defense & opened my mouth to respond: what came out was a memory. A banshee wail. Sixteen years of silence in that life & my first sound was a noise traveling across the ocean & across a century. A noise of grief.

My reward was that I hanged with them.

Over & over again   from life to life   my curse is a curse of silence. My lips have been sewn shut somewhere. & my voice always condemns me to execution. My voice: carried across the ocean. A banshee wail. From where?

The Irish people tell the story of banshees. The restless ghosts of women burned by the church as witches. Their spirits sliding up the stakes & consigned to wander: restless. They wander in forests. Swamps. Bogs. Places of wilderness not yet conquered. & they scream their grief in a blast of fury. A voice which heard will kill the listener.

Mainly true. But: we do not only lurk in swamps & forests. Sometimes in cities or countrysides. & we do not always choose to scream.

After all, I've thrown myself out of my body so many times. The silver cord slick in my palms as I pull myself out: hand over hand. Now the joints are lubricated too well:

> I jackknife out at the slightest shock. It has become worse with the passage of time. When I am shocked or angry. When I laugh too hard. If I trip or slip. Out I go: floating above the heads of the shocked bystanders who watch my body slump softly to the ground.

The doctor I saw about the problem called me: narcoleptic. So I have learned to suppress my own joyful urges. Reinscribed my own curse of silence. Causing my doctor to apply another term to my condition: melancholia.

Only these days one isn't burned at the stake for these things. Instead of the stake, instead of leeches to draw out bad blood I get: therapists. To draw out the soul. My secret ghost out in the open. Only the joke is: I haven't got one. I gave it up to the four winds.

But I know it is not gone. Only scattered out. To the planet. The cosmos. I too was scattered but managed to come back together. Ask anyone who has been on a sinking ship. They know: water like the soul   always seeks its own level. So perhaps one day my ghost will come flying back to me, wings fluttering, clucking apologetically. Without a word of explanation for its   at least three hundred years   absence.

1592. Irish hills. A town perched on the hillside next to a dark forest. A town square with quickly arranged benches.

For people to watch.   Me:

Burning.

I am gone before the body catches fire. Before the sullenly brown hair catches fire & is   for a moment   red once again. & then is ash. They watched me burn but did not hear me scream.

Telling my story is supposed to (*my nails are shattered*) help me untangle it. Yet each memory is (*the smell of hair burning*) loaded with others.

When the silver cord connecting self to body is knotted one's lives collide. I have no avatar. I cannot separate my self from myself.

Some part of my ghost remains (*across the ocean*) in each place I gave it up. So I am at once:

> a pilgrim: & the grandson
> of pilgrims.

One's dreams get caught, thick, in the pipelines of the mind. There is not enough space in them to allow free passage.

& the dreams lose their fluidity. They take real shapes. They lose their illusory qualities & become more than phantasms. Their presence is misread as prescience.

The dream juice has no more space to issue forth into new dreams. It stews in its source. The liquid dreams seep down into the brain. Causing madness. Or death.

Solution: widen the pathways of the mind through: art, poetry, painting, dance. Or: sift through the dreams with a dream-net separating the solid parts, the substance, discarding them.

I am incapable of art. I see everything with a purple cast. & everything seems to burn. My ears are tuned to dissonance. I am backwards of tone deaf: symphonies sound like cats in the alley. A lullaby sounds like a funeral dirge. An operatic aria sounds like an Irish banshee.

I tried dancing lessons once but with each leap & twist I popped out of my body & floated to the roof of the studio. The instructor shook his head in pity: narcolepsy, he said. Too bad. Such a young, small body could have danced well. It wasn't my body he was noticing: it was the restless ghost inside.

I have put together enough pieces to understand the reasons I died. Without purpose on the altar of an absolute. & perhaps then each time my birth was opposite. Born of ambiguity. Perhaps this is the reason I cannot remember them. Ambiguous cathedrals do not rise high enough in the dreamscape to make effective landmarks.

> I go sleepless tonight. Three hundred years or more since I flew up from the thrashing body on the rope. Four hundred years since I flew up the stake. Years since the eclipse burned the purple from my eyes. The moon—

that temperamental wanderer, causing men to turn into pigs or worse, rendering women into pain, rendering me deadly, bringing the tide boiling over the land, the serene moon

—passed in front of the sun & brought raw images into focus. Slowly giving me threads to pick at. To follow through the maze.

Earlier this evening as the sun dropped below the line of trees & the shadows draped taut on the ground I panicked.

& I could feel the weight of the rock pressing down on me. My rib cage cracking open this time. My heart exploding.

It's been five hundred years, I thought, weeping in pain: for the purple that was burned from my eyes. Not this time from another's fire or a badly tied hangman's knot but from my own immolation:

> staring up into the worst kind of eclipse: the moon passing only partially in front of the sun.

Yet still: who is that boy. With black hair. & purple eyes. Climbing the rocks.

Cries of angry men rising up behind him.

Behind me.

I, with purple eyes. I am running up the rocks.

& they are chasing me.

I begged my secret friends not to abandon their charms, their herbs, their magic books which had borne them across the North African desert on wings. Who would listen to me? A boy: sixteen. Yet still I talked.

Too loudly. & would be silenced.

By the time they caught me there was nothing left of my little shoes. Or feet. What fingers & toes weren't broken by my mad rush up the mountain they broke with their clubs. & silence me they did:

> a tanner's needle & a leather thong. Three held me down screaming while the other took that thick needle & pierced my lower lip. & stitched my mouth shut.

& the blood rushed into my forever-closed mouth. & I died there on the rocks. Under the hot sun. Drowning. The strings in my throat begin producing the last, long echo...

★

Having died once by each element: fire, air & water, I contemplate the fourth: earth. & know that the next death will be the last. That I must find him, my original self, the boy who drowned in his own blood, before I go into it.

Midnight & I feel the centuries square on my chin. The taste of blood thick in my throat. My lips itch to open.

The weight of the rock thundering on me. I lean down on my hands & knees & put my palms out on the floor. & think

> *through the floor, the concrete, the top soil & gravel, the water table, deep into the earth—*

> & I feel the rushing up. Suddenly: I am about to explode.

I can hear the hissing. & smell the smoke as my hair burns. My hair darkening now into pure jet black, the fire combusting into the air.

My eyes are bleeding out their odd godly color as I feel myself fill.

The sound of my beating heart makes my small bones sing.

There is something in me which will not let the earth-fire in. & suddenly I know what it is:

The restless wandering spirit which I had always thought lost. Sagged into some small part of me: the silenced part. The part that kills the magic.

I am weighed down with curses centuries old. Haunted by deaths which silenced me but did not end me, possessed by a willful & angry spirit.

The waves and waves of light-blood gush from my mouth as my lips blossom as if I ripped that leather thong loose, my mouth in shreds.

Light rushing into me and out of me. & my body throbbing like an earth about to crack open into space & the strange sounds of birds breaking & I: threaded deep now into this body, this life, giving up the ghost—

MORNING RAGA

- 1 -

Threaded seed to wonder.

Break the landscape at the window.

White paint peeling against the cerulean sky.

What did Alexander call it. *Wabi-sabi.*

He doesn't know what it means. It doesn't matter.

Metal murk and thunder.

And have you forgotten last winter when you stopped eating.

Still shifting in his seat, refusing to get out of the cab.

The surface of the black river still.

The surface of his face in the rearview mirror ash-filled still.

As the cab pulls up to the curb, Quinn watches the woman standing on the corner at the crosswalk, her eyes closed, her arms out either for balance or to catch some vibe from the air.

"I need new instructions," Priti had told Dimitra that morning.

"I need to give up my old habits."

Walking into traffic for one thing. Following birds that led her away from her destination for another.

"The cars are the same as me," she whispers. "The street is the same as me. I am the same as me..."

Quinn keeps watching. Her lips are moving but she doesn't step off the curb.

- 2 -

Memories lived as if in another life.

Quinn unpacking.

But it isn't about that; it's about leaving and Quinn does it best: always leaving something behind or taking something that doesn't belong to him, always arriving underfed in clothes that don't fit, with a scissors-in-the-kitchen haircut.

"When we were living in New Orleans," he says to Alexander, "my hair matted into dreadlocks and I used to stick small things in it. Pencils, bus tickets. A glass pipe."

"You can make a story out of anything," Alexander says, tracing letters onto the glass tabletop.

Quinn leans forward and kisses him on the cheek. "You are writing in gin on a table. You are the storyteller, not me. I collect trash. That's all. It's not very interesting."

★

Dimitra decides that Darwish was wrong, that you *could* draw the war on the walls of a city. "We'll stage music, performance art and poetry readings to protest the military interventions in Afghanistan and Iraq."

"And I'll dance in the streets," her roommate Priti says.

"Which would qualify as performance art," Dimitra agrees.

"I don't think it's a good idea," says Alexander.

"And Quinn can create a graffiti/trash archive of the city's responses," says Dimitra.

Quinn isn't listening. He is looking out the window at the patterns of the birds.

★

"An arrangement of strings," reads the score on the table.

Dimitra looking at it through the door. Yellow sunlight.

Slight taps. Rain at the window.

"Alex?"

Alexander bent under the piano lid, dragging quarters along the strings.

Obsessed with making new sounds out of old things.

Cage of glass, score scribbled on gin-soaked napkins.

Evening unrolling, yellow sunlight deepening.

Somewhere in the back of her mind the strange unhinged sound of piano strings groaning.

- 3 -

Seen: first the gray sky spread mercilessly down. Horn gray. River gray.

And birds—what kind were they?—black tears.

Marked as bruised arms, marked as the cut stump of a tree.

Marked as a tree rent by lightning. And he climbed inside. *Is this home?*

Dimitra in the doorway listening.

Here: the uncurling of days, the unbecoming sky.

Priti is helping Quinn unpack a box of books.

"I suppose it doesn't matter," he says. "They aren't even mine."

"Where did you get them?" she asks. "*A Short History of the Sepoy Rebellion. Understanding Cometary Phenomena. Tristram Shandy.*"

"I think that box was out on the street and I just grabbed it on my way out of town. Sometimes people write in them."

"This one has math equations in the margins!" she says excitedly, holding up the astronomy book.

Quinn is silent. She looks up to see him looking at her. Suddenly he reaches out, takes her chin, turns her face this way and that.

"No," he says then. "You are too used to being watched. I suppose you've been drawn too many times."

"I like being watched," she says. "The painter's eye is like the camera's lens. It's nothing, it's death, it's like self-cancellation."

Quinn knows what she means but does not say so.

- 4 -

The unstruck sound can be heard.

Alexander plays Cage's *4'33"* over and over again, sometimes with an open piano and sometimes with a closed piano.

These other times the wind.

These other times with open music.

These other times counting backwards and forwards.

Through the crated veil another telling.

Pass the curtains and derive the far equation.

He can't pick up any old trash and make it into something, Alexander reasons. He has to comb through trash piles and strategically choose things. That's why Dimitra said "trash-archive."

Music is like that: unfolding in space through time.

Trash sculpture unfolds in time through space.

Accumulating and accumulating.

So they *could* make something together.

- 5 -

Left to her own devices Priti might have left or written something on her own.

It's right through the window the arrow the driven.

Driven to remember, she recites: derived from percussive agenda its three beats on a drum.

Dance is a dialogue.

Form is more careful than memory. Sound of drum remands an imitative performance of preternatural symphonic choices.

Which goes against every grain: that the body should lead and the drum follow.

In the classical Indian system, after all, there are twelve whole notes, not eight.

A dancer whose casual moves derive from particle physics and cometary phenomena.

Given a choice, she might refuse to go along with choreography based on music or rhythm and rely instead on her own self.

- 6 -

Dimitra remembers Joachim's face.

She remembers the birds flying up into the persimmon tree, her eyes lowering, his body turning away from her.

"How shall I put my hand?" asks Priti. "Shall I close my fingers this way? It's called *chin-mudra*, the sublimation of the individual ego..."

Either way the wind drops down savage between the buildings.

To no one Dimitra asks, "Are you saying it is better for me to forget?"

Alexander raps his knuckles softly on the side of the piano.

As usual Dimitra is unsure whether he is performing music or "just thinking."

Priti twines a curl of hair in her fingers. "So you always leave a place. When you start to feel something for the people there. Well, what is it you leave behind each time?"

Quinn grows calm. Feels the sound of the ocean coursing through him.

Priti understands. "You aren't going to say."

- 7 –

A broken window.

Of water.

Finally the courage.

To take a shard and cut into the skin.

To fill the cut with ink.

Before: a piercing in his nose, in his eyebrow, in his lip.

A tattoo of blue wings spread across his back.

A boy flying high over the ocean.

Oh shine this way
Shine this way

Quinn by the piers remembering.

Through a shot glass Dimitra gazes out.

Alexander distracted by the look on her face. Staring in Quinn's direction but her eyes in soft focus.

She's looking through *him*—

And someone is singing in their mind:
Oh sign ocean sign and so the birds came to lift me…

Priti says, "How does all this go together?"

They are looking at all the scattered notes, choreography, musical scores and sketches of what graffiti Quinn wants to scrawl on the gallery walls.

"Why does it have to stick together?" Quinn asks.

The TV is blaring coverage of the war. "Warnography," Alexander called it. "Wargasm." They had to invent new words for it.

"I know it doesn't," she says. "It doesn't."

"You think it should," Quinn says. "Even after all this," and he gestures to the table full of paper. "Or that," and he looks over his shoulder at the television.

- 8 -

No time snowing down lightly into the earth, seeded.

No time to ember last summer, relentless, amiss.

How Joachim disappeared.

"He was mine before he was yours," Alexander reminded her after two glasses.

But now, shimmer of light, porcupous hill, scandal-monger, she wonders.

"A five-year-old Iraqi girl paralyzed by a cruise missile which exploded—"

"Stop," says Quinn.

Priti turns from the television.

"We have to get to work on this," he says, "or we will never be finished."

"What do you remember the most about your travels?" she asks him.

Quinn is not listening.

Night stretches like a tarpaulin. Stars turning in a wheel which in chronological time ought to take ten thousand years or more.

Know that the body and the spirit were woven together with energy.

What do you remember the most.

Not-listening.

- 9 -

"He was the angel of death," says Alex. They are on their fifth glass.

Dimitra pretends not to notice how close Alexander is sitting to her. She smells patchouli, sweet fennel…

Joachim: son of a French mother and Filipino father. Tall, swan-boned, fair-haired. And golden eyes like a wolf.

Alex imagines himself backward to him. But he was always Dimitra's. Not anymore.

"I did love him," she says. "I did. Still do, I suppose."

Wind, wind-throw, wind-know, west-left, left-retch, clef-sent, cleft—

★

—wind—windthrown—wind-eye—windwhy—

"Sometimes your life takes a left turn," Quinn says to Priti.

She doesn't stop dancing. She thinks if she stops he might stop talking.

Windtunnel, windrope, windopener—

"I didn't think I was leaving. I had to choose but I didn't know I was really choosing."

"Did you go back?" she asks.

But he can't answer because Dimitra came in with Alexander. She held a piece of paper.

"It's an anonymous note slipped under the door. It says we are unpatriotic and un-American and by staging our show we are subverting the war effort and supporting the enemy."

The walls of the studio were covered in white sheets. "I don't want anyone to see the graffiti until the actual opening," Quinn says.

Every time she looks at Quinn now she sees Joachim, though Joachim is taller, happier.

"Why are we even *doing* this?" she asks. "Why make drawings no one is going to look at? While we are being threatened. By someone in *this* neighborhood? I can't believe this could happen in New York."

Alexander turns the letter over in his hands. It is handwritten. Quinn takes the letter from him. "May I have this?" he asks Dimitra.

"Why even do this?" she asks again softly. "We're not convincing anybody."

- 10 -

Dimitra watches the dark birds wheel and streak through the gray sky of the parking lot.

"Joachim loved them. Because they leave no path."

"It's like music," agrees Alexander. "They appear in silence and then are gone."

Dimitra is transparent. Even as she declares independence she depends on Alexander's memory as well. Her mouth is full of Joachim's tongue.

She's barely aware that Alexander is speaking as they walk to the car. "It's not strictly true," he is saying. "There are no less than *seventeen* harmonic overtones the ear hears when a single note is struck..."

★

Priti lying on the floor of the gallery next to Quinn. Stars seen through the skylight.

"Then you forget," he is saying half to her, half to himself. "Years and years of this and you don't remember anymore what you said to who, where you left off, what you thought you were doing, where you thought you were going...

"And then it's years later, you've moved four times, none of your mail gets forwarded anymore and you think probably everyone you cared about along the way has forgotten about you a long time ago...

"The problem is that they're still brand new to you. You remember the last time you saw them perfectly. You still love them the way you always did. It hasn't occurred to you that it was nine years ago actually—

"One day you are cleaning out the canvas bag to go buy groceries and you find this receipt in there from three cities ago and you just think: *I have no idea who I even am...*"

Priti, counting stars, drifting tunelessly in half-sleep, suddenly realizes he has been talking to her—

★

"Everything counts," Dimitra says. "Everything is important. What we say. What we do."

"You're saying this because of the letter. It's handwritten. We can find out who wrote it."

Does she care who wrote the letter? The threaded landscape. The piano strings being scratched by coins. Birds wheeling in the sky.

"I'm calling Joachim tonight."

He looks at her then. Panicked. He doesn't want her to call. He doesn't want her to get to Joachim first. He doesn't want Joachim to hear her voice, after all these years, first.

Her fingers above the buttons on the phone. The long space between the tip of her finger and the small plastic square. She knows his number by heart of course.

Years since she's heard his voice, talked to him.

Wondering if she should call. Wondering why he hasn't.

And now, calling late into the night. Purposely leaving no time for talk. Just in case he should actually answer.

★

Alexander is rehearsing in his mind all the things *he* should have said to Joachim when he had a chance. He wants to snatch the phone from Dimitra's hand.

He turns to the car window. Plays back his score: found music, recorded sounds, conversation on the street, newscasts, a broom sweeping broken glass from the concrete, a key turning in a lock.

Quinn can make sense of it, he thinks, coldness in his stomach. Dimitra with her finger still hovering an inch away from the buttons on the phone.

- 11 -

Priti rising up on the swells of sleep on the gallery floor.

Written on top of writing.

All the writing collages, graffiti on the walls shimmering like the ocean.

"Is it even real?" she asks.

The diary she once kept on huge sheets torn from a pad of butcher paper. She rolled each one up and slid it into a mailing tube, sent each one to another Priti Krishna in a different city.

She told about her day, the ordinary things but also about the dances she invented, the people who came to see her. She wrote it as if she were writing in a diary to herself. In a way all those women *were* herself, she thought.

She imagined their faces, wondered if they had families, if they went to college, wondered what they were doing with their lives.

She looked up their street numbers in the phone book, lettered each tube and sent it off with no return address.

- 12 -

Dimitra hovers like a bird on a hot air current.

If I call what will I say if he answers?

Otherwise if he doesn't answer what can I put into my voice that will translate itself into the machine?

And Alexander:

How can I reach him after all these years, how can I remind him of how to love me? What words can I use to make him choose me?

★

The constellated swirls. Murks. Quinn sleeps. Priti runs her finger lightly over the graphite matte of words Quinn has slicked across every surface in the place.

A need to really say everything, write everything.

Then thinking: I want to leak into this.

He's given everything away, she thinks.

Not even close, he thinks.

★

This is how I imagine the ocean—

You've never been to the ocean?

Never.

I went in November. Ember. Remember.

This is what it feels like.

Careful.

Care fill. Fill me.

Full of you.

Storm on the ocean where no one sees.

I see.

Look at me while you do this.

Fill me.

★

She has to go across the widest space.

Her finger moves now automatically. It's okay, she says to herself. Just let your body do this. You just watch while your body does this.

This is insane. Why call him now.

Alexander thinks: should I stop her? He looks hard out the window.

She catches sight of his face reflected there. Looking at her, reflected in his window, with a look of panic.

And then someone answers. "Hello?"

★

It's this moment, Priti whispers to herself.

Standing still here.

While the music slowly evaporates.

And people shift from foot to foot watching a perfectly still body on the stage.

Music drifting to silence.

Minute after minute.

Watching each minute shift.

The lights don't go down.

And you sit there wondering if something is supposed to be happening.

THE PHOTOGRAPH

BENNY

Collin is staring into the photograph as if it is moving.

It's a man, his body, lying back in bed, his one arm flung behind his head, his chest open, with the other he holds a cigarette to his mouth. The sheets are rumpled. Someone has just gotten out of bed, leaving him there in the lazy afternoon.

He smokes.

When I visit a new city, and I've been in a lot of them, I always want to do two things first, even before unpacking, even before calling the people I am supposed to be visiting. I want to walk in the streets of the city, aimlessly, without purpose, with no intended destination. But eventually I want to look at art.

And Paris is a good city for that. I don't know anything about art, I will tell you, and that may be why I want to look at it.

I'm starting in the wrong place.

Let me start instead like this: It is always cold in Paris in November, but it is not the cold I mind. It is cold enough to have to wear a jacket and scarf, remind yourself you still have to take care of yourself, still have to keep yourself warm, remind yourself: you are alive.

When it's warm you forget: that a body is a vulnerable thing, that it gets older, can sicken, can disappear and die.

I wait for a minute but Collin isn't paying attention to me. His eyes narrow as he looks.

A photograph is only a moment. Written in light as the case

may be. Not a digital image captured and broadcast, but a chemical process, framed by the eye not the machine and the light written in water and solutions. Maybe that is what captivates Collin. He stands there, almost on his tiptoes, looking at the photograph. Me, I've never had much feeling for them.

I turn from him and wander into the next gallery where seven or eight people sit, hunched against the wall, big pads in their laps, scratching intently, peering at the giant canvases on the opposite wall.

It's all naked angels and Christians, nothing much interesting. But I want to look at the art lovers, look at them while they see something transcendent.

"*You're* transcendent," I whisper under my breath to the guy closest to me, a tough-looking kid with messy hair and big shoulders, gritting his teeth and staring at the painting. I turn to look at what he is looking at: three women—no *two* women and a very feminine dude—reaching up to Christ's feet. They've got a nail through them.

Flicking a look over my shoulder, I see Collin is still staring into that photograph. Pierced. That's the look on Collin's face. He's pierced. By what? Fear? Longing? Lust?

Why do people look at photographs anyhow? Or paintings?

I don't really come to art galleries to look at paintings. I come to art galleries to look at the people who look at paintings. And how they look at them. Some people drift through, looking here and there, never at anything for more than half a minute.

He looks up at me, the boy drawing. I look back. I don't look away.

"What are you doing?" he asks me.

"Same thing as you."

He tips the pad toward me. I see the figures are drawn but only in outline. He's not studying detail but composition.

"Okay," I say. "So it's not the same thing as you."

"What then?" He pushes his hair back but it only makes it look messier as it is sticking up in different directions.

"I am trying to remember you the way you are."

"Take a photograph," he says indifferently, turning back to study the painting.

I crouch down next to him. "That's not the same thing."

"Why?" He doesn't take his eyes off the painting he is sketching.

"Because it just reproduces. The mind isn't in it. The body isn't in it."

He looks at me for a minute. Puts his pad to one side then rolls up the sleeves of his army green jacket and turns his forearms up to show them to me. On his left forearm extending from the inner elbow to the wrist is a word written in Greek. On the right forearm another word.

"Are you Greek?" I ask him.

"I'm from Kansas." He smiles. I smile. He gestures with the left arm, "Eros."

"And?" I ask, pointing at the right.

"Psyche."

I wait.

"The mind and the body," he says.

"If that's what you're interested in, you know they aren't in a photograph," I say. I take his hand, the one he was sketching with. He is strong. "They're in the hands and on the paper."

"Who is your friend?" he asks me, gesturing with his chin in the direction of Collin. He leaves his hand in my hand.

I twist to look. Framed by the doorway, Collin is still there, leaning on his tiptoes in front of the same photograph. Even though he has a beard now, different than when I met him and something I can't get used to, he looks, from this distance, younger than he is.

"Just a friend."

What makes him look so vulnerable? I want to know. Is it the attention he is giving to the photograph?

"I'm in a class, you know."

"I figured."

"So I shouldn't be talking. You're distracting me," he said, taking his pad across his knees again.

"Do you like it?"

He smiles and holds his pen above the leg of a seraph. "I like it."

I make to get up, go back to Collin. Maybe we can find a bar near here and have something to drink against the chill. The artist puts his hand on my knee before I can rise.

"You can kiss me now."

Bold. I lean over and peck him on the cheek.

He shrugs a little but starts sketching. "Hardly what I was expecting."

"It'll have to be good enough," I say, standing up.

I leave him to walk back to Collin.

"Hey," he says before I've even taken a few steps. "What do *you* think the moral of the story of Eros and Psyche is?"

Uh-oh. Tell the truth or make something up? "I don't even know who they are," I call over my shoulder.

"At least tell me your name."

"Benny," I call back without stopping.

Collin is still looking at the photograph.

What is in it? I wonder again.

Are you Eros? I ask Collin silently as I approach him, looking at his face in concentration. *Or Psyche?*

I know photographs are literally created by a chemical reaction of light against darkness and then developed in a chemical solution. I don't remember the formula anymore, but it is one of many things, like the story of Eros and Psyche, that I learned in school and then forgot.

COLLIN

His face. Can't see it really. Light coming down from the window behind him. He's all eyes and mouth.

It's not that which makes him beautiful. Nor his arm, flung casually across the sheet, his chest open.

He looks away at someone standing out of the field of the camera's vision.

It's me or I want it to be me.

I look at the date. I would have only been eleven years old when this picture was taken. But if it could have been me, I would have wanted it to have been me.

He is smoking a cigarette, and he doesn't care that he is being looked at. Maybe he is so used to be being looked at that it's nothing.

But it's the nothing in his look that makes me want to fill him. With everything I carried in my hands here—a strangeness, a loneliness, but a love for that loneliness.

Why should I belong to anyone when I don't belong to any place?

I think they go hand in hand, the place and the people in it.

The photographs in a place tell you something about the people in it but not the pictures *of* that place.

And this photograph: of a face that is disappearing, a man that is disappearing.

When I first saw this photograph it was on a computer screen and I couldn't properly imagine it: how big it was or even that the man in the photograph was real, was flesh and blood.

This picture was taken twenty-five years ago. He'll be twice the age now than he appears in the photograph.

Is it grotesque what happens to our body, what we do to ourselves? Is that the crime of a photograph? Is that why we say it is *taken*?

SIMON

He leaves walking back to his friend. I roll my sleeves back down.

What was I thinking?

I wasn't thinking. That's Eros.

Now I'm thinking. That's Psyche.

And he only *looks* smart, hanging around art galleries saying all the right things about paintings versus photographs, but he doesn't even know who Eros and Psyche are. Dumb.

And dumber than dumb, he can't even read Greek letters.

Even fraternity boys can read Greek letters. And how hard are Eros and Psyche anyhow?

Still he had been looking in the right directions. He did want to kiss me. Eros.

Then why didn't he? Psyche.

Because his friend is right over there.

His cute friend.

His cute, strange friend who seems stuck in place in front of that photograph. I'll take a look on my way out of here.

The paper in front of me is just outlines. We are learning how to create bodies in space, measure perspective, their distance from one another.

The slightest space between two bodies can hold incredible energy, I remember reading. Erotic energy.

And psychic energy, I want to know. How do you measure that?

There is erotic energy between his eye and the photograph he is looking into. I shift so I can look better.

And who was it that said dumb is more beautiful because it is emptier? It makes space for you to pour yourself into.

Now I am like Benny, I think. Looking at the people looking at the art instead of at the art.

COLLIN

Benny and I went to school together. We met my first year of college because I was a young Christian and wanted him to go to a prayer meeting with me. How did I know his family was committedly secular and the only thing that could have been worse than telling them that I made him Christian would have been telling my family that he made me gay? Which he did.

But he went with me to Bible group week after week. One night, after a meeting, we stayed up late talking. The pastor had talked to us about homosexuality and sin. I didn't want to go home. When he went to use the bathroom I climbed into his bed and pretended to fall asleep. And then really fell asleep.

I woke up the next morning with Benny wrapped around me, his mouth on my ear.

I listened to the sound of his breath for about twenty minutes before I slowly turned around. When I got to face him his eyes were open.

"Were you awake?" I asked.

"I'm gay," he said.

"What?"

"Or I think I am. Maybe I'm not. But I'm definitely not ever going to be a Christian."

"I don't think I am either," I confessed. "How do you know if you are gay?"

He answered by slipping his hand into my shorts while kissing me.

Benny was not the first person or even the first boy I ever kissed but it was the first time it felt like how I always thought it was supposed to. Benny rolled over on top of me then, a little rough.

I was so tired. I wanted to be close to him. The warmth of his body, the heaviness of it, felt good.

"Benny," I said.

"Let me," he says, stroking my face.

I let him.

★

This past summer I moved to Paris, and Benny came in the winter to visit.

The city is cold and gray in November but Benny finds something beautiful everywhere. He is always pointing something out, going on about some historical figure or artist. I don't even know half the time if he is telling the truth or not but the stories are good.

Paris is hard for me because I left someone back in New York. Archie filled me, filled me with himself, his beauty, his strangeness. Archie stays up late into the night so we both stay up. Archie doesn't eat refined dairy or sugar or gluten so we both pick through menus endlessly.

The day before I left him, Archie drew a frame in my journal, said he would draw a picture of us together when we saw each other again. He left me with the blank.

Maybe that's what Archie is to me still, after all the time we've been together: blank. As successful as he is, as beautiful, he stays blank. I used to think it was because of his family. They're Indian, and I don't think they ever really understood why their precious Arjun dropped out of med school. That was almost worse than being gay for them. Almost. At a certain moment, I stopped thinking it was his family and started thinking it was just Archie himself.

So I came to Paris alone to work as a writer for a tech website. To Benny's endless frustration, I don't even *like* Paris. It's not much of a city—kind of cold, gray a lot, the people are nowhere near as interesting as in New York. Here's a dirty secret: Paris is *boring*.

But Benny turns Paris on for me. He keeps trying to take me places in the city from his previous trips here but every time we get lost. And then there's nothing to do for it but find a little art gallery, look at some beautiful things and then go drink some wine.

Blank and still unsure of what I am doing here, I feel not quite bored but remember how with Archie I barely had to think—

125

he cleared everything away, demanded in his quiet way all my attention. I willingly gave it and so slowly disappeared.

I had to leave New York, come here alone. Finally alone, maybe to really figure out who I actually am.

This show though. Frightening. Nan Goldin. Of gay men in New York and Fire Island during the middle and late seventies. Meaning: most of these men are dead now.

And this particular photograph—a man reclining on the bed, nonchalant, shone in sunlight, recumbent in the rumpled sheets, smoking a cigarette, diffident—this one I have seen before.

I look at Benny. He is talking to one of the artists in the next room. Benny has a type, I realize. He likes scruffy guys; that guy looks a little unwashed, a little underfed. Pierced, skinny, dirty.

He made an exception for me, I always knew. It was a sweet thing, that morning, really, like a little gift he was giving me for being able to say I wasn't Christian anymore. For being able to ask him what I asked him.

I never talk to Benny about God because there is too much explaining to do. It seems to me that there has to be one if for no other reason than a real God, not a new-agey, celestial, omnipresent happiness, but a real God—an old man in a robe sitting in the clouds looking down, aware of the tribulations of the earth but for some reason, some agreement, unwilling to intervene except in random cases—seems to be the only counterbalance I can imagine for the flimsy, forlorn, delicate and dangerous human body.

Where are you now? I ask the photograph of the man, though, like God, I know exactly how to find him if I want to.

BENNY

We leave the gallery and walk into the crowded foyer of the museum. Collin isn't talking about the photograph and I am not talking about the guy with the sketchbook. We know each other well enough and for long enough to leave each other alone sometimes.

I loved Collin once, when we were younger, when we were kids really, but not anymore. He exhausts me, the way he looks straight at a person, tries to see inside. But I know: what's inside him frightens him so much he has to pay attention to everyone else.

And then Collin starts talking.

"Sorry I dragged you here. There was a reason. The photograph."

"The one you were looking at the whole time? You didn't even see the other ones."

"Neither did you," he says.

"I know," I admit. "I found other parts of that gallery equally attractive."

"I've seen the photograph before."

"Really? Where?"

"On my computer."

I stop. He stops to look at me. He is standing close to me, afraid the people around us would hear him, I guess. For the first time in a while I am the quiet one. Waiting for Collin to start talking again.

COLLIN

His photograph was beautiful. "Written in light," that's what they say, don't they, that the word *photograph* means in Greek?

He lay back on a bed, one arm thrown over his head, resting on the palm, casually—with his palm facing out—smoking a cigarette. He was inhaling, a look of naked hunger on his face. His arms and chest were thick with muscle, light flooding the room, his eyes focused sideways on someone who must have been standing to the left of the photographer, perhaps in the doorway to the room.

I fell in love with the photograph. I wanted that strength, that carefree, unapologetic hunger, to be lying in bed in tangled sheets in what's clear is late afternoon light, sticky with sex and nowhere important to be, no work to be done.

He sent me a message on a hook-up website. His picture opened itself up on the screen. I saved it onto my computer so it would always greet me. We talked for a while on the website but not in ordinary tongues I don't think. We would talk back and forth like wind does to rain. He was funny, strange, savage, desperate. I would ask him questions and he wouldn't answer.

★

Where do you live?
Sometimes I don't know, other times New York.
Is it snowing there?
Snow feels so cold and good on my face.
Where do you like to spend time?
Anywhere there's natural stone. I have to drive up the river and find it.
Why stone?
So I can actually be here and not think I am going to disappear.
Why are you afraid of disappearing?
Mountains are more permanent than bodies. Bodies die.

Are you sick?

Not sick really. But.

Um what do you mean.

A lady never tells.

Tell.

Sorry, didn't mean to be cryptic.

I want to know.

I've had HIV so long I don't think of it as strange anymore. Even though I haven't told many people and I don't even know what you look like or your name and I told you.

You know what my chest looks like and my mouth.

Not the same thing.

And my cock.

Sure.

And my name is Collin.

Collin. Collin. Yes, Collin, your name feels good in my mouth. Two L's.

Not the usual way.

I could fill your mouth.

That would be nice.

I like your photograph.

Thx.

Where is it from.

When you mean.

Or that.

It was a long time ago. 20 years? A photographer came to Fire Island and took pictures of all us kids who were living out there, raising hell. She's kind of famous now. Who knew?

Sounds fun.

Fun. Maybe. Yes it was. But most of those guys are

Not alive anymore?

Not alive anymore.

★

I knew anyhow that he didn't look like his photograph anymore. How could he? But time was what I had. Archie was working and

I told him that I was going upstate for a couple of days. I wrote to the man on the website and told him I would meet him downtown somewhere. I can't remember if it was he or I who suggested the Chelsea Hotel.

I caught the 1 train downtown.

The whole time I was dreaming of Archie. To be touched, kissed, fucked by him. I've known him for ten years and he still looks exactly the same to me, still as young and beautiful as when we first met. And one is willing to do anything to burn when one has no fire oneself. But Archie's fire was a cold burn. He held me at arm's length always. Sometimes I'd lay awake all night next to him, wanting his body. He'd wake in the morning and without even saying anything, he would give me the briefest of squeezes and head into the bathroom and start showering. I'd reach around for anything—a t-shirt, a pair of underwear, a sock—that smelled of him, press it to my face and release myself.

I felt safe on the train, rushing underground, away from Archie, to some neutral place, away from his strong body, his beautiful arms, his face somehow more handsome with slight lines from age, his remoteness, his casual cruelties.

The fog-laced river raced past. Archie is the one who taught me everything, how excruciating the body's ecstasies can be. But I can't breathe under his there-ness, his presence.

Twenty-five years had passed since the photograph was taken so I knew the man would look different. I was prepared for that. He had been dark, terrified, but also funny in our conversations, flirty.

We agreed to meet at the bar in the basement of the hotel, and I had booked a room for the night. The light was already darkening when I got to the bar. I walked in and saw him in the corner, leaning back. He was thinner—skinny even—and had lost the muscle in his arms and shoulders that made him such a rock star in the photograph. He had a hungry gleam in his eyes. Hungry for me, I think.

He was fixing his glance on each person who walked in the door, I imagine, trying to guess which one was the man coming to meet him.

This time it was me. I walked straight up to his table.

"You're Collin," he said.

I sat down. I didn't ask him his name.

His face was drawn and his cheekbones sharply etched with lines. I knew the look, the look of men who had received the first generation of HIV medications, medications that not only made them sick of a sort but ravaged their beauty and aged them.

He drank his beer. I ordered gin.

Was there beauty in an aged face, was it more beautiful than a youthful, smooth face? I loved Archie's beauty, rangy, his hooded eyes.

Or is age really just a movement toward death? In the case of my not-yet-lover's death, a movement faster than any other person I knew.

He wasn't at all anymore the man from the photograph. He was thin enough that the skin of his face and around his collarbone looked draped a little bit on the bone. He was talking incessantly. He must have been drinking for a while before I arrived. I couldn't focus on his conversation. He leapt from one topic to another. Maybe he was coked up as well as drunk.

My gin came.

So his beauty was gone. That's not the point. His face was haggard, his body skinny, but he was still the same man I had chatted with, going on about his new jacket, a friend who was opening a new night club on Seventh Avenue, a small cottage he was thinking of buying upstate in Sullivan County.

I drank the gin quickly and said, "Let's go."

He either liked me being bossy or he was too drunk to complain because he paid our bill and we went out and climbed the dark central stairs to the second floor. He put his arm around me. I put my arm around him. He was so light, hardly there. We walked down the dark hallway, barely lit by small yellow bulbs.

We were about halfway down the hallway when he turned to face me, dropped to his knees on the carpet and started fumbling with my belt.

"Hey, don't," I said, trying to pull him up.

He held on to my legs tight and looked up at me.

"*Please,*" he said. "Please let me."

Looking down at him I wondered: *Is this how Archie looks at me?*

"Come on," I said, extending my hand to him. "Get up, let's go to the room."

He pulled my shirt up out of my pants and kissed me lightly on the skin just above my belt buckle. "Okay," he said.

We walked the rest of the way hand in hand. I was turning the key in the lock when I started crying. What was I doing here? I imagined Archie at home working and I was here in the dark, with a man who maybe was sick and could make me sick and he was trying to get into my pants and I was going to let him.

It was then I knew I had to leave Archie. Because I didn't care if I caught something. It didn't feel important enough to me to care.

Suddenly I was tired, tired of romance, tired of using my body, tired of what I always thought of as the connection between sex and death. It was like he was dead already or I was and I didn't want to know that sex and death had something to do with each other, after all my Christian upbringing, all the shame that had ruined me.

We went into my room and he collapsed immediately onto the bed and fell asleep.

I packed my things quietly and left him a note saying I had checked out and that he should sleep as long as he wanted in the morning. I stopped and looked at him still sleeping there. I wanted to take his clothes off. I wanted to kiss him. I wondered if I should take another photograph. Then there would be two: the young and beautiful body, desired and desiring, the other one, aged, ravaged, ruined.

BENNY

I stare at him. He is looking off down one of the gallery halls. He doesn't want to look at me. I see something in Collin I haven't seen before, a toughness, something fierce.

I don't know what to say. "Did you write to him again?"

"I didn't," he says. "I haven't looked for his profile either. I don't want him to know I am looking for him. I don't know if he is still alive."

"I want to look at the photograph," I say, turning, but the guards tell us the museum is closing soon and so we can't go back into the other galleries.

"I've looked on and off for the photograph but I have never been able to find an image of it on the internet and it has no title so it's not exactly searchable. Today is the first time I have seen it since then."

We wander through the museum to the exit. "I've never told anyone else about this," Collin says. "Not even Archie. You have to promise never to tell Archie."

I promise.

We go out into the street and walk for a couple of blocks to a restaurant Collin knows that serves raclette with boiled potatoes and cured meat. I have shaved beef. Collin eats charcuterie.

"What was it like," I want to know, "when you first walked into the bar? Did he flirt with you? What was he wearing? What were you more turned off by, his sickness or his desperation?"

"Well, that's the thing," Collin says, "I *wasn't* turned off. If anything I wanted him more. Seeing what he used to be, how he'd changed. And his desperation—it was *arousing.*"

As Collin talks, I watch his mouth, his lips, I remember what it was like to hold Collin, remember the smell of his hair, the feel of his cheek against mine.

Collin's phone rings. He answers it and then looks at me once with surprise. "It's Archie," he says and jerks his head to say he is going outside to take the call. He leaves me at the table.

I sit at the table for a little while looking at Collin's empty chair, unsure about what to do with the feelings I am having for Collin. I eat slowly, wondering where we would go from here.

Collin comes back to the table astonished. "I can't believe it," he says. "It's too perfect."

"What happened?" I ask. He seems confused and amazed at the same time.

"It's Archie. He hasn't been feeling well. The doctors ran lots of test. Including HIV."

I wait.

"His test came back positive."

We pay quickly and leave to walk back to his apartment some blocks away.

"I'm the one who had been a lot riskier. I must have it too," he says. "I must have been the one who gave it to him."

"We'll go tomorrow," I promise him. "We'll find a clinic and we'll get a test."

We come to his apartment and go inside. He opens a bottle of wine.

"It's because of that photograph."

"I thought you said you didn't let him."

"I didn't, but it made me braver. To be with other people. I thought I was being safe. Safer. Whatever."

"How does Archie think he got it?"

"He doesn't know. He said he didn't do anything. He said a couple weeks ago he met a guy who blew him in the bathroom of a bar. Can you get HIV from that?"

"I don't think so."

"Archie's uncut."

"Maybe then. I don't know. I guess you could. It sounds wrong."

"Maybe the hospital gave it to him," Collin says.

"It's kind of fucked up that we know so little about all this."

Collin jumps up and pushes the little table aside. I grab the wine cups before they spill. He pulls down the Murphy bed onto the floor. "Get in bed," he instructs me.

"What?"

"Take your shirt off," he tells me.

I pull my shirt off.

"Your pants too," he says.

I drop my pants and step out of them. I climb into the bed. He tears the sheets loose and rumples them around me. He puts his hands on me. He moves me where he wants me to go. He manipulates one arm overhead, puts a pencil in my hand to act as the cigarette.

"Suck on it," he says. "Breathe. Look that way. No up a bit more." He cups my chin and moves my head so I am looking in his eyes.

A long time after my lust for him had turned to love and then love had turned to friendship, he touches me in a way that brings all the old feelings back. He steps back and looks at me in the frame of his hands.

"This is what it was like," he breathes.

I already know, growing colder in the sheets, looking at the blank eye of his camera, I already know the story between us is over. Collin isn't going to choose me, lying in his bed under the small skylight, cold in Paris. Collin is going to go back to the ruins of his life with Archie, back to the memory of the ravaged lover, the sick one.

When he climbed into my bed when we were kids, I put my arms around him. I have never wanted him since then. Only now that he is shadowed in danger and grief, putting his hands on me, moving my limbs, trying to recreate the photograph.

C O L L I N

We sit in the small reception room and wait our turn. We have to fill out forms in French. Benny keeps telling me what to write. There are three or four other young men waiting with us. Each so beautiful I want to just disappear with them. What am I about to find out?

The bored receptionist, the one who took our forms and corrected Benny's French, comes to the door. "Collin," he says. I get up and follow him. He is wearing a metal-studded belt, the kind of belt I always want to wear but never can; I wouldn't look stylish, only silly. He holds a door open for me. I go inside.

Another man is waiting for me with a clipboard and a syringe. And thank God the man speaks English with me.

"Why is it you want to get tested?"

"I have had unprotected sex with someone who recently tested positive for HIV."

"How recently did you have sex with him?"

"A month ago."

"Were you the active or passive partner?"

"Um, passive."

"So you think you may have given it to him?"

I don't answer. He takes out the needle. I see the needle, thin and silver, like a road between one life and another life.

It is one thing to help Archie through something. But what if he gave it to me?

Its cold point on my skin. And then the needle goes into me.

BENNY

"And why do you want to get tested?" the man asks me.

"Mostly to support my friend."

"So you have not engaged in any high risk behavior recently?" the man asks me.

"No," I lie. "But it is better to get tested and make sure, right?"

"Yes," he agrees, uncapping the needle.

COLLIN

I put my suitcase down in the hallway and listen. No lights, no sound. I go into the sitting room, and there in the window, I can tell by his outline, is Archie.

"Hey," I say.

He turns. Backlit by the streetlamp. I can't see his expression. "Collin," he says in that low, fevery voice of his.

I approach him. I can smell the flowery shampoo he uses on his curly hair. Is he crying?

"Why are you here?" he asks, turning away from me.

All my old anger comes back hard. Why turn away? Just to be dramatic. Why *ask* me why I came? Isn't it all obvious? But that's Archie, wanting everything spelled out, wanting everything on his terms.

And then I stop myself. He *is* crying. I put my hands on his shoulders, then slip them around his thin waist and bury my face in the flower scent of his hair. "Of course I came. Why would I not come?"

"What's going to happen to me?" he asks me.

"You have to talk to your doctor. You can deal with all this now. There are lots of treatments."

"Did you get tested?" he asks me.

"I went with Benny to get tested," I say. "We came back negative."

"Then it really is my fault." He turns away. "I was almost hoping it was you that gave it to me. Is that awful?"

"It isn't. It's everything. It's all the pieces in the world that moved in a certain way."

"We want our lives to move at the speed of sound," says Archie, "and then you change."

"You haven't changed. Your blood has something new in it. This isn't a plague, Archie. It's not your fault that you have it."

He does not answer.

"It is not going to kill you. And you don't deserve to die. Why are you buying into all this bullshit?"

"One day you wake up and what you thought was going to happen to you didn't happen. Your blood changes. You aren't who you were."

Now I am afraid. "What are you trying to tell me?"

B E N N Y

Weird because I came to Paris in the first place to visit Collin and now he's gone and I'm still here. It is a cold but bright morning when I catch the train down to the Père Lachaise Cemetery. I wander down the rock-cobbled avenues under that peculiarly beautiful late autumn sun that seems to get more and more yellow the colder it gets. I don't take a map, I don't know where any of the famous grave stones are, though I pass Frederic Chopin by accident and Marcel Proust as well.

As I turn one of the corners I see a big crowd gathering in front of one of the graves. There are some news cameras as well. I walk closer. People are standing in small groups waiting. There is a podium set up. The tomb is a massive concrete cenotaph, sterile, blocky, ugly. Along the side of the crown there is an art deco angel, its wings posed behind it. Oscar Wilde.

On the podium is a photograph of the same cenotaph but covered by, ravaged by millions of dark red and pink lipmarks. I join the crowd. I recognize the guy I'd seen that night at the gallery. He is standing next to me, wearing a green corduroy jacket and a black newsboy hat pulled down over his ears, sipping coffee out of a paper cup.

"Hey," I say nudging him, as if I'd just left him a couple of minutes ago. "Where's my coffee?"

He smiled back. "Oh, yeah, I forgot yours." Sips again. "It's so not French to take coffee to go. You had no idea what it took to get them to give me this cup."

"It's so much better to sit on the street and sip though, isn't it?" I ask him.

"What, and miss this?"

"Yeah," I say. "What exactly *is* this?"

"*They,*" he says, stabbing his thumb in the direction of a group of suits standing near the podium, "are forcing poor Oscar to wear a condom. No more barebacking."

I put my arm around him, my hand on his shoulder. I pull him in toward me. He leans into me, resting his shoulder against my side.

"People would come here and put lipstick on and kiss the stone. The grandson of Wilde who controls his estate felt that it was a defacement."

"Wilde had grandchildren? Wait, Wilde had *children?*"

"He said it was damaging the stone sculpture."

"It's an ugly statue anyhow. It looks more beautiful covered in kiss-marks."

"Garish, isn't it?" he asks, his lip curling over his teeth in a wolfish smile. "And that guy," he points to a taller man with a black beard and beautiful smile, "is here to legitimize the proceedings."

I recognize the actor from his many film roles.

"Do you really want to stay for this?" I ask my friend. One of the men had approached the podium and microphone and was calling for attention.

Simon is fumbling in his book bag. He pulls out a little tube of lipstick.

"*Merci d'être venu*," the man at the podium says and the reporters and cameramen focus their attention on him.

Simon applies the bright pink lipstick to his mouth.

The man begins to speak. I understand enough French to follow a little bit of what he is saying. "In order to preserve the dignity of Oscar Wilde and to protect the valuable sculpture donated by the artist, we have decided—"

He is interrupted by the sound of Simon stepping past the barrier and kneeling in front of the plexiglass sheathe. All the cameras turn and begin snapping photographs of him. He leans forward and planted his mouth against the glass and left a large and glaring mark there.

Turning to the cameras he blows a kiss and says, "You can't put our boy back in jail."

SIMON

After talking to about three newspapers, two radio stations and a TV station, I finally get out of there. I thought the organizers were going to kill me, but it was pretty awesome pissing off that movie star. Though I'm pretty sure *baiser* means "fuck" in French and not "kiss." So I said to that TV guy, "Everyone has the fundamental right to fuck Oscar Wilde's tomb if they want to." Oops.

"You were awesome!" Benny cries, catching up with me.

"Oh yeah?" I ask him.

"Yeah," he says, grabbing my shoulder and spinning me around to face him.

"You move a little quick," I say.

"Tell me to stop," he says, putting his arms around me.

"I didn't say that," I say. "Where's your friend?"

"He had to go back to New York. He got some news from home." He looks at me. I thinks he is going to kiss me again. On the mouth this time. I wonder what he would look like with pink on his lips.

"Listen," he says, smoothing my hair back.

I wait.

He doesn't say anything. He leans forward. I close my eyes. He kisses the lids. He kisses one cheek bone and then the other. He holds my face with one hand, opens my scarf and leans forward and kisses my throat. He takes my hands palm face up and kisses the center of each. He rests his face in my palm. He cranes my neck down and kisses my forehead.

"You don't even know my name," I say.

"Spend the afternoon with me," he says.

"I know a place near here that serves *vin chaud*," I say.

"I'm thirsty," he agrees.

A R J U N

Collin is gaunt in his blue suit. His eyes so tired. Why should I say anything.

I feel I am already disappearing. There's nothing left of me to listen to him.

He touches me but I can't feel his hand on my shoulder.

He is speaking but I don't know the words, only these sounds in the air.

Outside the sky is orange turning gray then blue on the other side.

I know orange and blue are the same.

My body with HIV and without it are the same.

I stand up. Collin looks surprised. I can't hear him.

I stumble toward the door. I say I am going out but I feel like I am speaking underwater or through time.

He looks at me as though from far away, as though he is looking at a picture of someone he used to know.

I want to go down to the street and be looked at by strangers.

Strangers look right through a person and see themselves.

Stumble and faint. Who am I?

Mimosa. Hot streak. Crayon sunset. Fox-flower.

Why Collin, why me, why now?

Bluer then bluer, the edge of the banister. Each step down. The door swinging open.

Walk toward me. Memory pool. Surf prayer. Sky swoon. Azure unraveling.

Seen. What is in my blood. Seen. Through the dark door.

I take off my night-jacket. Through the haze and wild. Fuck me.

CORRESPONDENCE

Dear Joachim,

It's all equal to you. I can imagine you:
sauntering. Dreaming your life. Why do I
think of the word "languid" in connection
with you when you were nothing like that.
I remember you standing at the edge of the
pier in the storm. Everyone was shouting
at you to come inside. It was the first time
I had seen lightning strike down—so far
across the water we couldn't see, they were
all hollering, and you, lanky, extreme,
beautiful, your hair going wild in the wind,
screaming into the storm.

Later when I read the expression "teeth
of the storm," I thought only of you,
carnivore, wolf, sweet killer. Teeth you had.

Listen, Quinn's gone and I don't know
where he went or what happens next. Have
I failed at the making of music, or at least
the making-it-count part. You're still there
in New York, in the heart of exciting life,
writing and making things happen. I mind
my daily lesson plans, face my classes, lift
the conductor's baton and teach this way.

But how to say what truly excites me about
music? It's this: today I was crossing the
street to come home, and a young man—

ten years younger? fifteen years younger?
Not really a man actually, but not a boy
either, as tall as me, broader, but still a
boy—crossed the street from the other
direction. We crossed at odd angles. Our
paths did not cross. Our gazes did not meet,
I gazed only barely at him and then back
down at the street, gray, but graying blue
in the oncoming twilight.

Joachim, how can I explain it. There was no
encounter, yet our strands came so close to
weaving and also not. I don't know where
he was going: I was going home, tired and
worn out from working. I had a meeting
with my department chair who wanted to
change my class assignment, wanted me to
teach basic theory to incoming students.
But how to describe music of leaves falling
from the tree, as wild as they are falling
now, yellow and outraged.

The season's edge is shearing itself now.
Autumn means to flutter away like tracing-
paper cut from the frame after packing.
You'd think I'd find a metaphor other than
painting. We both know where that's going
to lead.

Just dreaming about the same thing: when
we were younger, had more freedom to do
what we liked, had less somehow. That's the
odd part; we had so much less.

Your hand less my hand. Teeth of the storm
traveling down my back. What's next?

Yours,
Alexander

Dear Joachim,

Yesterday. Music in the rain hitting the windowpane, the shingles. What doesn't matter. William tried to explain to me that matter doesn't go anywhere. That all the matter that exists in the world has always existed. That it only transfers into and out of bodies.

You and I could have once been another body. Another body the same. I would like to make a symphony of all the sounds in the world. All the atoms are striking each other but all the atoms have been one another. William says there is a theory in physics dealing with this but I can't wrap my head around it except in metaphor.

Ironic because as a musician I have always wanted to break the systems, have always envied you, Joachim, because you are a poet, a novelist, have always been able to write whatever words you liked, whatever worlds you liked, given alphabet and syntax but honestly with the freedom to break each.

Don't you sometimes open the skin and dream it. An open ear or an eye closing. A series of photographic shots up and down the street. A guest book of an artist's exhibit. Conversations overheard at a funeral home. I only dream it through you. But you take it to dream.

Do you envy me my shapes? I have these to work with: time signatures, predetermined key pitches, the same twelve tones everyone else has to work with, and unless I want to invent more, these specific instruments.

So maybe I will play one for you: play the surface of the water. Play rocks and paper. Play scissors against rock and paper. Play my voice. Play a cough against traffic. Play the wind across my mouth. That's song.

Song the afternoon evening. Is that night to you? Do you want to know what spells night to me?

The dark ink on the staff paper. Here's a clef for you: Alexander sitting in the coffee shop on a Saturday morning. Across the water the huge rock protrudes into the river, soaring thousands of feet over the town. In afternoon its shadow stretches nearly all the way to our side. Lengthens and lengthens, runs through the streets and darkens them before true twilight.

Alexander listening to the radio music being broadcast in the café, drinking his coffee and reading Gertrude Stein's weird lecture notes. She at least understands there is the possibility of *actual* music in the words not always in the meaning. But wanting meaning. As being a child and hiding in an excellent place. Wanting to be found.

Found Joachim, you're going to write this one day into smoke or into my skin. My smokescreen. My clumsy bowing across the sky. Me as Odysseus trying to unstring the strong bow of the sky.

Yours,
Alexander

Alex

Look both ways when you cross the street,
friend. I can imagine you now, one ear
cocked to the sound of the world you
always think you're hearing. Bird music,
tree music, you're music, Alex, don't you
get that part?

Last summer I went to France to visit my
cousin. We tooled around Paris for weeks,
hitting every museum we could. You hear
that Paris has many museums, but you don't
even know, Alex—I want to go there one
day with you, I really do. And do all the
stupid typical things with you. Kiss you in
the rain, all that.

This time I hardly had any money. When I
left New York, I emptied my bank account
and cashed it all into francs. I had a couple
thousand and we decided to go south and
just hang around until I ran out of money.

The *auberge* in Cassis was three miles up in the
mountains. You had to hike up the rock trail
and follow little symbols and signs painted
onto the rocks. There was a collection of
people up there, Alex, dissidents and rock
stars, artists and students and ruffians and
refugees. I met a beautiful Belgian, sleek
like a sylph, with the eyes of a thief and
the fingers of a pianist. He didn't tell me
his actual name but his stage name: Mister
Stevarius. A fire-eater.

There was a professor of some kind up
there too with his blacksmith girlfriend. He
talked about Harryette Mullen. She made
lime fizzes for us to drink.

You finished college. You got away from
Joel. You got yourself together. Who
thought you ever would? Don't get down
on this being constricted by responsibilities
or being trapped by things. Listen—actually
forget what happens next: just listen. It's
what I do: listen to the world around you,
the conversations that happen, the music
that happens, the sound of the ground, it's
talking to you, Alex.

How do you think I write but by trance? Or
by chance? Have you ever listened to John
Cage, Alex? Listened to what happens when
you don't plan, don't listen, but throw dice
up into the universe? You can't imagine.

I imagine you in that coffee shop, under
the shadow of that mountain, practically
weeping because you hear in the wash of the
words and the streets and the sweet sweet
coffee your music. I get that you hear music
in that.

It's enough that you hear that and you
wish you could write it down. It doesn't
really matter that you can't write it down.
A traveling road, impossible, scary between
you writing it down and then the years.

Soon there will be a man—disconsolate
and desperate maybe—it's morning in
Washington, DC, and he's walking to work.
It's summer so the air reeks of manure and
magnolias and there is a book on a street-
side table and maybe he's interested by its
size or smallness or the feel of paper or the
size of type. Maybe he takes it. Reads it.
Maybe he doesn't. On his shelf for years.
Years, Alex, before, having nothing else to

read, he starts it. Gets drunk on it. Can't
believe he's lived so long without having
read it. Actually believes he *has* read it,
though must have been years before since
he can't remember.

It's like that with you and Stein, isn't it?

When I got home I looked at the little poster
Mister Stevarius had given me. Incredible
pictures of the man, shirtless and divine,
breathing fire, the little efreet. There was
a small website printed on the bottom of
the poster. He writes of himself, "Mister
Stevarius: a poetic figure. Here I breathe to
you the frightening fire. Will show you the
transmutation of the soul's lead into gold."

Can you imagine a fire-eater who sees
himself in the true way: an incredible
alchemist. A transliterator. Pronouncing
fire into an unspeakable alphabet of gold
and the soul. Really unbelievable but you
have to meet the man, so earnest, his eyes,
Alex, his eyes.

So what matters this time is you're stretching
out where you don't know how to write it
down. Don't you know by now your life is
good enough, that you're holding this music
inside you, that you're gifting the world,
gifting with breath and breath and breath?

Do you believe me?

Joachim

Dear Joachim,

Last night the rain continued, continued.
Water in a circle through: from the ground
into the air—in the air there enacted to
storm. Storm you Joaquin running in music
now to the earth across the lake—so wide
we couldn't see the land except by where the
lightning strikes. Then a river from the sky.

Faithful. Do I believe? I believe. Leaves
listening on the sidewalk, on the roads,
coming in storms now—October turning
into November. Later—after the rain, after
the morning sun, the leaves have been blown
from the walk, but there remains a ghost
of the rain-soak giving their silhouettes.
Little fingerprints of rain.

So I fell down into sleep. The rain was
around, wrapping itself in the sound
of it. Like the drone in Indian classical
music. Shall I add rain to the repertoire of
instruments for my new symphony, shall I
call it "unfinished" because that way anyone
who listens can add in anything they like:
run the shower, slap their hand on their
belly, something funny like that?

But for some reason language and music
swelled in my sleep, came back up like the
ocean, roused me up. Lines kept running
through my head, and some corner of my
mind kept telling me to roll over, get my
notebook, write it all down. I was borne
up—you understand that you cannot
drown—*cannot*—unless you swallow water.
The notes and phrases bore me back up to
the surface of wake.

All the stories of my life, orange flowers.
The window panes could crack in their
casements.

Here's the city in the dead of night
whispering, whispering.

Me, accursed, hearing bass tones perfectly,
could hear the snores of the old man who
lives in the apartment next to mine. His
snore cut through the walls, cut through—
and I couldn't go back to sleep, even after I
had written. I turned a fan on, I turned on
music, I put earplugs in my ears and tied a
scarf around them, yet still—

So that's my funny story about hearing
too much, hearing too well. It's not just
symphonies and poverty, not just your
raving poems and your funny strange little
novels, it's not just you and me wishing
we could be together again, but also this:
the spilled soup, the leaf-circles drying in
the morning, the old man's snores quiet
to anyone else but to funny Alexander an
absolute outrage.

So I haven't slept in weeks it seems. I can't
imagine what Paris would be like or even
New York right now.

Alexander

Dear Joachim,

You want me to confess it. Why I'm writing now all of a sudden. Why we are both trying to avoid the subject. Why should I be the one to go first?

Do you remember in college—during the snowstorm. You were living with Quinn, this would have been right after we met. You writing a symbol on my hand and not telling me what it stood for. You holding my wrist, the silky feel of the brush on my shoulder. Your breath against my neck as you concentrated.

Who cares that I chose Joel? You had me first. Touched me. Wrote on me.

I tried to find you a couple of years ago. I tracked you down on the internet and found out that you were working as a chef at this little restaurant in New York City. The manager at the restaurant wanted to know why I was trying to get in touch with you. I said I was a "friend" from college. When she asked my name I gave the name "William Trask"— I don't know why I didn't say my real name. Probably because I thought if I gave my real name, you definitely wouldn't want to talk to me but that if you thought William or Dimitra was looking for you then you would answer.

Well, we know where that went. Years more of silence on account of my strange fear.

There's a museum here called the Dia and in it are all kinds of contemporary artists. I mean really cutting-edge stuff—

it fits the stereotype. For example there
is one sculpture that is in its entirety a
huge mountain of broken glass. I am not
kidding you. Big shards sticking up out of
there. The crazy thing is, if you look at it
long enough you actually begin to see the
sculptural elements in it. Is that crazy?

Every time I go there I find something that
appalls me. And so I stay and stare at it for a
while until I figure it out. There's one room
for this artist On Kawara. He takes canvases
and paints them completely with black
ink. Then stencils in white with perfect
regularity the day on which he makes the
painting. That's it. No variation, nothing—
except that sometimes the background
painting is dark, dark blue. Some days
there's more than one painting—two and
one day there's three. Can I explain it to
you? No.

But as I sat there staring at the dates I
looked at the dates that framed the time
we were all at college together, you, Quinn,
Dimitra, and I, William, Joel, everyone else.
Everything we held in our hands those years
came back to me, Joachim. Everything I
let go of. Tell me, is all of that lost? Has it
gone completely?

There are things I do not believe.

The train is going by just now. I am putting
the sound of it in with this letter.

Alexander

Alex

Every practice has a death. My yoga teacher tells me that all the time. It probably means something more significant. But I think you need to get out of that place, Alex. You're coming apart.

Last night I was lying in bed with Siana and I was telling her about you. About these letters that are suddenly coming out of the air. Arrows from the past. They're from this Alex who I don't even know anymore. And of course you're not *you* sending me these letters. You're *him,* Alex from before. You're twenty-three, fucking beautiful with those big coffee-cup eyes of yours and that crazy rock star hair, as stupid as you are beautiful.

I don't think this is real, Alex. I don't think you actually want to go back through all that time. But I wanted Siana to know everything. Who you are. Were. Who I used to be. Am.

It isn't how you think it is. Working for hours—your boredom that loops you like a cloud-net. Have you seen Cecilia Vicuña's cloud-net?

Listen to me avoiding telling you what my conversation with Siana was like. But why should I tell you, Alex? You're a dervish, you're the spell-binder, you're the one who pulls music out of traffic, rain-storms, you're spending your life listening to a mountain, Alex. It's *legendary*. You only really remember me because of the way I used to make you feel and because Quinn's gone.

I am, I confess, completely lost. Haven't
been able to look at this newly. There was
a dream I had last night of lifting up to the
ceiling, or being lifted. Do you still keep
your dream-notebook? I have to balance my
checkbook. The temperature here dropped
nearly 20 degrees overnight. You have to
get out of that place, I'm telling you.

A while back there was a phone call and
Siana answered it and she asked if anyone
was there and waited and no one answered.
When she told me about it later, the person
I thought of was you. That you had called
and she answered and you got afraid and
didn't want to talk.

When I think of music, I think of your
voice.

On top of the cold, there's really bad wind,
chapping my skin and lips. First that phone
call and then a letter. In the mail. From you.

It's okay to leave things unfinished, Alex.
Household chores, raking leaves, grocery
shopping. You're the art lover. How many
works of art do you know that are so
brilliant exactly because they are unfinished:
they complete themselves: a couple of
brush-strokes on blank canvases, a novel
that contains the same word in terrifying
contexts, or is printed backwards, music
that doesn't stop but just drifts away, sky-
writing and wind…

Joachim

Joachim

Yes it was me that called and I couldn't say anything, I couldn't.

Beautiful and stupid, how flattering. Is it wrong to think that all that time is still alive, that you are still on my skin, that I could wake up in the middle of the night to the sound of the door opening and someone coming up the stairs and sliding into bed next to me and it's you, you somehow.

It doesn't seem fair that we come back to the same *places*—look at me living on Willett Street again, in the same building and teaching at the same school we tore up—but that time doesn't come back.

Only my mind understands, but my body keeps waiting for you. I will leave the door unlocked. Just come, just get in the car and drive. Don't tell me you're coming. Just walk in one day or else climb into bed while I'm gone out during the day and wait for me or just come in the middle of the night while I'm asleep and climb into bed and wake me up with your hands on my body and take me, take me without asking, take me like I belong to you, because I do, I belong to you, I always have.

Alex

Joachim

Are you not writing back now that I have
done what you asked and gave you the
honest

When anything can be said one is drifting
on a wind-river

If you paid no attention to form you could
swim too

I feel like I opened my mouth like you asked
me to

So put something in there

FOOL'S ERRAND

1

ACE OF SWORDS

Qays finds himself in trouble, unsure of himself again, unable to speak even a syllable of Catalan and having just enough Spanish vocabulary to order a second cup of coffee.

Besides which, if the clouds do not disperse soon, the Mars-Venus confluence won't be visible at all and his trip to Barcelona will be a waste.

TWO OF SWORDS

Qays was fourteen when he first turned to face the sky, watched its dark linen shredded by glittering sentences flickering down, brief phrases, glistening once and then fading.

These are not unbound bodies drifting across space, he knew, but objects seized by the earth, plucked from their travels, hurtling down.

The first time Qays kissed a boy it was one year later, in the hot August evening, while the Leonid meteors littered the sky's margins. He brought a friend from school out to the field to watch.

As the other boy explained that what they saw were not heavenly bodies but actually rock and dust, Qays seized his hand, pressed his lips quickly against the other boy's cheek, the sudden well of desire exactly equaling the explosion of shame in his heart as the other boy shuddered and pushed him away.

THREE OF SWORDS

Qays was given a pad of blank star-maps and a backyard telescope by his uncle for his fifteenth birthday and over the next five years he pored over every season's sphere, marking systems, movements, unexplained phenomena—stars, quasars and comets all carefully delineated in his brisk and sharp penmanship.

In love with the dark, he worshiped the sky and touched no other person.

FOUR OF SWORDS

Qays needs to know if it is going to be clear in the city tonight. If the sky isn't going to be clear from Montjuic or Tibidabo then he can go to Montserrat and see the sky from there.

The waiter, who Qays has been trying not to stare at since he came in, is walking by. Lacking the language to call for his attention, Qays reaches out and takes the lip of the man's pocket with two fingers.

When you came in here, thinks the waiter, you were like another planet discovered in the solar system. "Your change is two euros forty," says the waiter in English.

"I have to check the internet," says Qays abruptly.

Your fingers are inside my pocket, brushing my leg. What could you want?

"I need to know what the weather is like, whether the sky will be clear tonight."

A man who is as passionate about the sky as one can be about a blank canvas or page or the sea, any empty space…

FIVE OF SWORDS

The waiter looks at Qays, then looks down to Qays' hand, still clasping his pocket. Qays drops his hand. "I'm sorry," he mutters.

"Why do you need to know the weather?" the waiter inquires, cocking his head to the side to look directly into Qays' face.

Qays, burning with shame for his enthusiasm, is closing his notebook, gathering his pencils and pads into his satchel. "It's nothing," he says. "Is there an internet place near?"

"I have a phone—if you want, you can use it." The young man holds out a small phone.

"Thanks," says Qays, taking the proffered phone without touching his hand.

SIX OF SWORDS

Qays leaves the café and walks through the narrow streets of the quarter to the courtyard in front of the cathedral. Something about watching the restrained, calming, subtle dancers there makes him feel less lost.

And also more lost, he realizes, sitting on the steps looking over the crowds and crowds of people in the evening light, holding hands in their circles, stepping first to the left and then to the right, raising their arms briefly, then dropping them again. He keeps waiting for a climactic motion, but there is no climactic motion.

It is like the waves at the shore. Or, he realizes, like looking at the sky. A quiet night spent gazing into the depths of black, the literally infinite depths of black.

They asked Us to make the spaces wide between them, he recites from the Quran to himself watching the slow and circular dance, *and so We scattered their stories with a terrible scattering.*

SEVEN OF SWORDS

During the flight to Barcelona, Qays had kept turning over in his mind things to say to his cousin, Nour. "Are you interested in science?" he'd asked her.

"Not really," she'd confessed.

"What subjects are you studying at college?"

Nour had looked down at her hands.

She bores quickly, Qays had thought, reaching for the airline magazine.

"Actually, Daddy doesn't know that I changed my major from accounting," she'd said.

Qays had become interested.

The flight attendants had come with their cart, dispensing drinks, coffee, pretzels.

Qays had ordered ginger ale. Nour had wanted tea with milk and two sugars.

"What did you change your major to?"

"Music."

Qays had whistled.

"I know. I'm asking for trouble," she'd said, taking a sip of the tea.

ACE OF WANDS

If there is an unstruck sound, I am hearing it all the time, Ash whispers to himself without opening his mouth. Inside my body there are a hundred voices whispering to one another.

He leaves the restaurant at the end of the night to walk into the twisting streets of the Gothic Quarter. His astronomer—his slightly peaked look, fidgeting around for his books on the table—stays in his mind.

But he didn't notice me at all, Ash knows, didn't even see that I wasn't hearing him but reading him instead. He puts his hands in the pocket around the phone, imagines it still warm from the other man's hand.

How will I find him again in the whole city? Ash wonders. The man had been worried about the weather. He wants to be able to see the stars. Ash will have to go to where one can see the stars in order to find him.

TWO OF WANDS

The sky turns blue then deeper, heading to black. The lower part of the crumbling wall in front of him, Ash knows, is Roman, ancient, rising from beneath the streets, from the city under the city, the city no one saw.

Made nearly deaf by illness and not by birth, Ash had a very hard time learning sign language and it was harder still reading mouths but eventually he did learn. He has, on the other hand, gotten very good at reading the physical gestures of others. For example, by the way his astronomer took his phone, made his call, then gathered his books and left, he was making a concerted and difficult effort not to look up at Ash at all.

When people speak normally, Ash can figure out their words by the very little he can hear. When people, like his astronomer, mumble, Ash can piece it together by context, gesture and emotional expression.

Ash drifts through the city not in utter silence—he hears things happening directly next to him as if they are happening fifty feet away, he hears things happening fifty or a hundred feet away—the music coming from the cathedral courtyard where the crowds are dancing the *sardana*—as if they are happening five hundred feet away—loud sounds muted to the extreme.

All things tending to silence. The way Ash watched the astronomer walk out the door without saying anything, without thanking him for use of the phone, without asking his name.

ACE OF COINS

Nour and Qays have breakfast together each morning on the small
wrought iron balcony off of Nour's hotel room. While Qays goes
out to buy bread and some fruit—nectarines, blood oranges—Nour
brews coffee which always comes out stronger than Qays likes.

In his absence Nour likes Qays more. She remembers interesting
things he had said to her, for example on the plane he'd said he
thought it was a great idea to switch majors at college. But when
he is present, more often than not, he is moody, uncommunicative,
focusing all of his attention on little chores—peeling the orange,
wiping crumbs from the table, slowly stirring sugar into the syrupy
coffee.

"Today I need to do a little research," he says to her. "Will you
be all right on your own?"

"On my own? Of course," Nour says, not sure how she will get
by even though her Spanish is better than Qays'. "I have to shop
for gifts for everyone back home anyhow."

Qays grimaces. Is it a sneer of disgust with her? Or is he just
wincing in the bright sunlight?

TWO OF COINS

When Nour was nine years old, as with every Muslim girl, her daily prayers changed from being a treat she offered her parents to prove she was a good girl to being an obligatory responsibility.

No one asked Nour what she wanted, but she didn't mind since she had always been able to read what the people around her expected of her and her ambition to succeed, lacking external direction, adjusted itself to never disappointing the people around her, whether it meant always having Dad's cup of tea ready for him exactly the way he liked it as soon as he came home from work or cleaning the kitchen after dinner without being asked.

She went a little extra distance by praying her Noon and Afternoon prayers as well as her Sunset and Night prayers separately rather than lumping them into pairs the way most people did, though this was partially to compensate for the fact that she never managed to wake before sunrise for Morning prayers and had to pray them *khazah* when she woke with the light.

There was an equivalent to everything—any prayer you missed had to be made up, if you missed a day of fasting you had to provide a certain number of meals for the hungry in order to recompense.

And if anyone worried about the chances of her cousin, Qays—who did not perform daily prayers at all after he turned fifteen, the age of obligation for boys—to get into Heaven, Nour took comfort in the *hadith* "One hour of study is worth sixty years of prayers."

But she doesn't know if what Qays does really qualifies as "study." What does he ever do but look at the sky?

THREE OF WANDS

Ash keeps his eyes on the path in front of him. He finds himself so easily distracted when he looks at the people around him; the lack of sound makes him focus all that much more on motion.

He remembers when Alex showed him motion could be sound.

Alex put his hands on him as if his was the body of an instrument—gently, on the sides of his ribs, turning him slowly around so his back rested gently against Alex's chest. He sat at the edge of the bed, between Alex's legs.

Alex kissed the left side of his neck, then leaned over and picked up the violin and bow. "Now take this," he said loudly in Ash's ear, which Ash could discern the edges of.

Ash's bare back against Alex's collarbone, the soft breathing in and out of Alex's belly against the small of Ash's back.

"My Ashwin," Alex whispered, which Ash heard only as wind, as he positioned the instrument more snugly against Ash's thin shoulder, took Ash's right hand in his and lifted the bow up into the correct position.

"Are you ready to hear?" he asked again loudly, and Ash nodded.

THREE OF COINS

It doesn't matter to me, Nour thinks to herself, walking down Las Ramblas with Qays towards the sea, the sky and whatever happens in it.

"Do you know the universe has a sound?" Qays asks her suddenly.

"Really?" she asks, pretending interest. Why can't he ask about how I feel, what I'll be doing today?

"It does. A galaxy millions of light years from here is emitting a note. A real note," he says with excitement.

"It's amazing," she agrees, wondering which note it is.

"There's poetry and science in the sky," he tells her. "And music."

In spite of herself, Nour smiles. "Qays, why don't we take the funicular car up to Montjuic? You can see if it is high enough to see the stars from. We could just—spend the afternoon walking around the gardens up there."

Qays looks at her a moment, his mouth opening to say no, but she is smiling, hopeful. "That sounds really nice," he says.

FOUR OF WANDS

From the Miramar Gardens, Ash looks out over the cacti and into the sea. That day Alex moved the bow against the string still shivers in his bones along the surface of his skin.

His skin and the wind.

The jacaranda lining the plaza reaches in every direction and Ash doesn't know which way to walk back down the mountain. On a day like this, cloudy but warm, he feels it harder to hear, easier to see—every color ramps up brighter in the gray storm-light.

Alex played the violin roughly with Ash's hands and he felt music going through him and throughout him in ebbs and bits. He wanted to sag completely into Alex but knew he had to keep his arms firm and torqued in order to keep the tension necessary for the friction of hair against string that would release the sound.

There is a statue of Mary—goddess of the sea—in the center of the plaza.

The sea, the sky, sound, the expressionless face of a distracted stranger or the impossible memory of an afternoon long finished when he felt sound in his bones, spent with a lover long gone—Ash has to choose which will be his god.

FOUR OF COINS

When Qays and Nour crowd into the funicular car with the other tourists, Nour tries to negotiate a position next to Qays, but he isn't paying any attention to her at all, so transfixed is he by the sea, glistening with white bars in the brilliant yellow-white light of the Mediterranean sun.

She keeps trying to catch his eye in order to share her experience of the diminishing city with him, but his back is to the buildings. All he cares about is the expansive blue.

Nour turns back to the city, watching buildings, cars, bicycles, people get smaller and smaller as the car climbs higher and higher on its cable towards the mountain.

I'm always alone, thinks Nour.

FIVE OF WANDS

At the Miramar Gardens, the sea an impossibility of blue and white in every direction, the city only incidental, ravaged by light, ravished by it, Ash sits on the great bulbous roots of one of the ombu trees lining the path. He leans back against the trunk, feeling its roughness on his spine.

What does the memory of Alex matter anyhow? Alex had been savagely tender and, sometimes, just savage.

Approaching and retreating footsteps and voices sound like the world is a sheet that is being rumpled in the wind.

As Ash tries to imagine himself after the fire of Alex burned through him, across his skin, deep in his bones, he becomes aware of another sound, in his bones, in his spine, more particularly in the tree he leans against.

He can hear a woman's voice in his bones, the way the sound of the violin had resonated in the body of the instrument and in his own.

For the second time he hears something not with the absent space of the ear but with his actual flesh and blood.

FIVE OF COINS

Nour compensates for Qays' silence by speaking, filling every space with news from back home, ideas for sites to visit next in the city, advice for Qays if the weather continues to be cloudy at night. She is leaning back against one of the ombú trees, flipping through her Barcelona travel guide, while Qays looks up, as always.

"It won't be cloudy tonight," Qays says, looking deeply into the blue above them. "I am sure of it."

"I think we should go see the Sagrada Família Cathedral, Qays. Do you realize the roof isn't completed—we can look up from inside and see the stars from inside!"

Qays' sudden desire to be rude in the face of her naiveté is cut short by his own intrigue with the idea.

"Do you think they would let us, Qays? If we asked?"

It's the first time she has shown interest in his true reason for being in Barcelona.

"I don't know," he says. "We could ask. Probably not."

It seems unimportant to explain to her that even if they were inside the cathedral they would not have a proper angle to observe the planetary confluence even if they were able to take in a telescope of enough power.

ACE OF CUPS

There are only five places in the house that Qamar can go and not feel the thickness of the absence of her husband strangling her—the landing of the basement stairs, the first floor bathroom, the laundry room, the guest bedroom, and in front of the kitchen sink, looking through the big picture window across the yard to the beginning of the foothills.

The small prayer room, added to the design of the house when they had it built, is one of the places Qamar can no longer enter. The smell of incense, the white sheet pulled taut against the floor, bookcase full of sacred text, images of the Kaba on the walls—

And her other son, Mikayl, did not pray. Qays was the only one who ever went in there anymore; since he had gone on his trip the door stayed closed.

At the beginning, Qamar had found it convenient that she had five other places to choose from which to pray and so rotated her daily prayers among them. But as the days went by, she found herself less and less interested in praying to the silent God beyond her house. If there was God then He was in here somewhere, she had thought. Maybe in those rooms into which I am afraid to go.

Qays' bedroom is one of the places she is afraid to go. Her strange, older son, moody and sullen one minute, voluble and frantic the next, looked at her with longing stares. Like he had done something wrong and was begging to be caught.

Now that he is gone she knows she can easily go inside his room, open his drawers and learn everything. But whenever she thinks about it, the image of Mulawwah comes to her mind, smiling and shaking his head. "Leave him, *na,*" he used to chide her. "He is our special *bachcha;* everything about him does not need itself to be explained to you!"

Of course, she thinks, crushing the explosion of grief that is blossoming in her gut, I can't even go into my own bedroom either.

The morning Qays and Nour left on their trip, Qamar moved into the guest room and stopped doing her prayers.

TWO OF CUPS

Two mornings after Nour and Qays leave, Qamar wakes disoriented. Looking at the speckled ceiling for a moment, she thinks she somehow managed to sleep through the night—finally—in *their* bed.

As she turns on her side, she sees the digital clock and knows immediately she is across the hall in the empty guest room. Five o'clock. Though she cannot bring herself to spread the prayer rug on the floor any more she still cannot break herself of the old habit of waking before sunrise.

"I should do the dishes," Qamar says to herself aloud, another one of her newly developed habits, along with the shocking inattention of leaving dishes in the sink overnight.

"I'm alone here now," she says, going down the stairs. Qays overseas, Mikayl away in New York on a school trip.

She stands at the sink, looking into the blackness of the yard and then the desert. In a few moments, she knows the dark will change to black-blue, then deep midnight blue, and that soon the sun will come up over her, in her empty kitchen, cleaning it.

"There's no one here now," she says again before beginning work.

THREE OF CUPS

When Mulawwah knew he was dying—not the first time, when the cancer was diagnosed, but the second time, after the first round of chemotherapy that worked, after the second round that didn't, and after the third round was helping, but only a little—he asked her for one single thing:

"You must get Qays settled. He is a loner, *na,* he doesn't really know how to do things the right way."

"It's true," Qamar says aloud, drying her hands and blinking in the now bright sun pouring through the window into the kitchen. How does it happen—that Qays would have to go all the way across the world to look at a planet when the Earth rotated around every day. Oh, Qays had explained it a hundred times how it happened, the angles of space, gravity, all the physics of light. "But you have to admit," says Qamar to herself, "it doesn't *really* make any sense."

"And Qays really *doesn't* know how to do things. Remember all the bounced checks from when he was in college? Coming in the mail every week. And his shoes!" Qamar laughs. In his twenties and a college graduate, Qays still cannot tie his shoelaces on his own and has to wear sneakers with Velcro straps.

"He calculates the positions of the stars but he cannot tie his laces," cries Qamar in mirth, laughing suddenly, her laughter filling the kitchen, filling the house. So loud for a moment she doesn't hear the doorbell ring.

"Who am I expecting?" she asks, with a curious mix of apprehension and excitement that there might be an unexpected guest at the door.

Through the muslin curtain she can see two outlines. She opens the door. Two extremely dark and very well dressed women, each holding a black book, stand on the porch.

"Hello," says the taller and younger woman with a big smile. She has a beautiful accent, Qamar thinks. African? "My name is Mrs. Evelyn and this is Mrs. Miriam. We have come to talk to you about how to have joy in your family. Do you have joy?"

Qamar's knuckles whiten a little on the door frame.

SIX OF WANDS

Vibrations can be felt through the ground itself, knows Ash, because he is sure he has felt them before.

Sounds of a truck rolling by two streets over. Sounds of a storm over the sea even when he was in town, a mile away from the shore. The sounds of a violin, through Alex's ribcage into his spine.

So through the trunk of the tree he hears a woman's voice, a woman who is leaning against the tree on the other side, spine to trunk to spine. He feels her in his bones. He can't help the odd rush of lust that travels from his pelvis up his spine and into his mouth. Suddenly he tastes Alex, tastes him on his tongue, the taste of cigarettes and beer that has never been disgusting to him, but arousing.

The woman is talking about sacred spaces. He leans around the tree to see who his partner in wood is.

And there standing in front of her, making small acknowledging words, but not looking at her, not looking at her at all, instead looking out, looking out over the edge of the Miramar to the sea, is his lonely astronomer.

She is still talking, but Ash, no longer leaning against the trunk, can't hear the vibrations. If he strains he ought to be able to hear her even though she is speaking in a different direction, but his blood is beating in his ears too loud.

They are speaking in English, that much he can tell, and his English isn't great but he tries.

"For this first time visiting Barcelona?" he asks them.

They both turn to look at him then.

Is that a flicker of recognition on the astronomer's face? Does he recognize him from this morning? Just a tremor in the mouth, nothing more. But Ash doesn't think the astronomer had ever even looked at his face throughout their exchange at the coffee shop.

"You don't remember?" Ash asks the astronomer directly. "This morning at the coffee shop. I served you. You don't remember?"

Another twitch. A movement in the throat as if the man is swallowing. Do they understand him?

"I heard the talk about Sagrada Familia. You want to go to the churches? To hear all the sounds in the open spaces? Then it's not Sagrada Familia you want to go to but Santa Maria del Mar."

"It's not sound we want to hear," says the astronomer then, thickly as if dazed, unconsciously speaking with Ash's odd grammar, "but the sky we want to see."

Again the sky. The emptiness which is not empty. Soundless and full and so Ash thinks automatically of its earthly counterpart.

"Then it's not Santa Maria you want to go to," amends Ash, "but to the sea itself."

SEVEN OF WANDS

"Oh, can we, Qays?" the woman asks in a burst of excitement. "To see the stars above the sea!"

Qays. So he has a name.

"My name is Ash," he volunteers. "You are from India?"

"From Pakistan," says Qays shortly.

"Pakistan, India, almost the same thing," says Ash weakly, trying to make a joke. They don't laugh.

"My name is Nour," she says. "How long have you lived in Barcelona?"

"Five years," he says. "For school first. Then I stayed."

"We came to look at the sky," says Nour.

Ash looks at Qays, waiting.

"The planets are coming together," says Qays. "And this is one of the best places on the planet to see it."

"And that is why you wanted the clouds to part," Ash says.

Qays nods.

"And look," says Ash, taking the chance to drape one arm around Qays' bony shoulders to gesture to the sea and the blue sky.

At his touch, Qays shudders hard. Ash flinches too and nearly takes his arm away, but Qays does not move or shrug him off. He stays there, timid, stock still, a frightened animal. He doesn't want Ash's arm there but he also doesn't want to move.

Ash looks straight at Qays' profile, sees the scared man darting his eyes sideways, trying to get a look at Ash but pretending to look out at the sea.

EIGHT OF SWORDS

Qays feels as if there is a sword cutting through him. Ash's arm is resting lightly on his shoulders. Nour is there, sitting just a foot or two away from where he stands. To shrug the arm off, to shudder again would be such a strong reaction. It is only a man's arm on his shoulder. It doesn't mean anything.

He tries to look directly at Ash's face. In his panic he has forgotten what Ash looks like, just has a vague impression of dramatically large and black-irised eyes.

He is afraid to move even an inch because he does not want Ash to think him skittish and lift his arm. He wants to rest lightly under Ash's arm but he does not want Nour to see how it makes him feel.

Suddenly, on the top of the hill overlooking the sea, for the briefest of moments, the sky doesn't matter, the sea doesn't matter, the sword cutting through him doesn't much matter, only this man's arm resting lightly on his shoulder.

Lightly and deceptively resting, Qays knows, because he understands Ash too is pretending, his arm laid so casually on Qays, he shifts it so slightly every now and then, just to make sure Qays' body is still alive there, still breathing, hasn't turned to stone or smoke.

FOUR OF CUPS

"Why do I need to tell them I am already Muslim?" Qamar asks herself as she arranges teacups, a sugar bowl and a creamer on the tray. "Didn't Mulawwah always say, 'All rivers lead into the same ocean?'"

Of course, what does that even *mean?* she asks herself silently, lifting the tray. Even though Mrs. Evelyn quoted multiple passages from the Bible to her, even though she hadn't understood, she wants to prove to someone, to herself, to those women, to any neighbors who might have been watching, that she is kind.

And strangely, she wants somehow to let Qays know that she is doing this, that she has opened the door to strangers. Strangers who now sit in her living room, their white-stockinged legs crossed, their Bibles in their soft hands.

"I made the special *masala* tea," she announces to her guests as she walks in. "What *these* people call *chai*."

Qamar realizes that she does not include Mrs. Evelyn and Mrs. Miriam with the rest of the Americans. When she says "American," she knows she means "white."

"You are a kind woman," says Mrs. Miriam, speaking at last. She gestures at the calligraphed Arabic writings on the walls, "And a spiritual one as well."

"We are Muslim," says Qamar then, serving the tea, feeling though that there was a little bit of a lie in the statement since she has not in fact been praying.

"It is a wonderful religion," says Mrs. Evelyn, sipping the tea. "And what a gift, this tea!"

"Do you feel happy then in your relationship with God?" asks Mrs. Miriam. "Or is there something else in your heart that you are desiring?"

Qamar stares past Mrs. Miriam, her cup frozen halfway to her mouth. Mulawwah stares at her from his photograph on the wall, those hooded eyes, that half-smile.

The door to the prayer room is slightly ajar. She has let something in. She exhales a small whimper.

FIVE OF CUPS

There's nothing here that belongs to me anymore, she thinks to herself as Mrs. Evelyn continues talking, quoting from the Bible, and pointing upwards every now and then with her finger.

All of these things I shared with Mulawwah and none of them are mine. Is that why I can't breathe in this house? Because there's no air in it?

Every day she tracks her sons moving farther away from her. Mikayl spending more and more time with his friends, coming home late at night, his clothes soaked with the smell of smoke. "I don't smoke, Ma, but some of my friends do," he would say.

She would hardly have opened her mouth to reprimand him when she would hear Mulawwah chiding in her ear, "It is not right to judge, *mere jaan*. Smoking alone does not make someone *haraam* and praying only does not make someone *paak*."

And Qays: Qays had been vanishing before her eyes, she can finally admit. Vanishing for years.

"When you have the body of Jesus in front of you, you have someone to love, someone to talk to," says Mrs. Evelyn. "Don't you sometimes need a friend who is right there with you?"

"Yes," Qamar nods, tears coming to her eyes. She doesn't know anything about Jesus but she knows she wants Mrs. Evelyn to keep talking.

As the woman goes on, Qamar fusses with the cups on the table. She thinks again about Qays' room, left alone now for two weeks. Mikayl won't be coming home for another day.

"When you go inside yourself," Mrs. Evelyn is saying, "you will see the truth that has been there all along, your friend is waiting for you, He is waiting just for you."

SIX OF COINS

They have come down to the beach. The sea spreads out before them, horizontal and endless. Nour feels that when she stands with her back to the town, with nothing at all in her field of vision but the expanse, she can see the earth curve.

Qays, at last, does not crane his neck up but stares with wonder instead at the horizon.

"Everything's real," he breathes in wonderment.

"Real?" Nour asks. "What do you mean?"

"In space nothing is real. The light that reaches you is traveling from so far away, you don't know what's real or not real, what's still there or what has long since disappeared into dust. But here at the sea—there's the water, there's the sky. It's *real*." He smiles and puts his arm around Nour, hugging her to him.

She nearly flinches at his touch but controls herself. Once the feeling passes, she tries to relax next to his warmth. But it isn't real, Nour knows. The water in the ocean and the air are barely separated. All day and all night long they are evaporating and condensing into one another. And the horizon—the horizon is not a place; there's nothing there.

"I have to go in," shouts Qays, pulling his clothes off.

Nour watches him strip down to his undershorts and run wild into the warm water. She allows herself one brief rivulet of lust watching him run, and then she knows, she knows she is ready.

SEVEN OF COINS

As Qays runs into the sea, the other boy, Ash, he calls himself, comes to stand beside her. He too watches Qays frolic at the shore, then jump further into the water, wading out to where the waves are higher.

"Your cousin seems happy to be here."

"We hadn't yet come to the beach." Because Qays was too busy with his science, she does not add. "What kind of name is Ash?"

"It's short for Ashwin."

"In English, 'ash' means what's left after you burn something."

"Maybe I have been burned," he says, and then she turns to look at him.

"Me too," she finds herself saying.

"By him?" he asks, pointing to Qays.

"No," she says, a little surprised. "Maybe. Well, by everything." He is confused but listening. "By my father mostly. He wants me to study business and be a Good Girl. But I love music."

He smiles. "I love music too even though I can't hear well. I dated a musician once. Who taught me to hear through my bones. A violinist. A beautiful musician but not a very happy man."

"Man?" she asks, surprised. "You like men?"

"You didn't know? I thought you knew—"

Suddenly, the waves are making her feel sick to her stomach.

"I'm going into the water, too," he says then, pulling his clothes off, and running toward the water.

Nour sees Qays, far out, the waves washing over him. The distant figure turns and spots her. He lifts both arms up and waves to her. Her smile, the one she's always flashing, feels false. Suddenly she feels like it has always been false.

She waves back.

EIGHT OF WANDS

The water is warm on his skin as he wades to where the astronomer floats, gazing out toward the empty space of the horizon. They are far out, past all the other bathers. The sky is a brilliant blue. The sea seems white around them, glowing.

Qays turns halfway as Ash approaches, sees it is him and turns back to the sky. Ash floats alongside Qays, just a foot or two away.

"I feel I have been here before, floating in this water, staring up at this sky. How can I be here? How is it I didn't drown? I think last time I drowned."

He leans back and floats in the water, letting the water cover his eyes, his mouth, leaving only his nose above the surface. He comes up, the water trickling off his face, his mouth.

"I want to live," he mumbles, speaking to himself.

"What?" asks Ash.

Qays turns toward him, reaches out with his hand, his fingers dripping wet. "We are so close in the water and so far away. Do you know that in the sky a star can appear to us as if it is right next to another star but in truth it is millions of light years apart from it?"

"But I'm right here," says Ash, sliding right next to Qays.

Beneath the surface their bodies touch. Warmth rushes through him.

"I want to live," repeats Qays, this time clearly, looking right at Ash.

NINE OF WANDS

"Then live," says Ash, drawing his stomach against Qays' stomach, his chest against Qays' chest.

"I'm afraid," says Qays, trembling a little. Ash wraps his arms around him.

He's so thin, I can feel all his bones. Qays is still speaking. And then Ash realizes he can hear him. When their bodies are together like this, floating in the water, Qays' voice is so low and smooth, his body so bony and fleshless, Ash can understand Qays without looking at his face. He can *hear* him.

"You don't understand what it is like," he is saying. "How complicated it is, what my mother and father expect of me."

Ash pulls back to look at Qays in the eyes. "I can hear you," he says in wonderment. "When you speak I can hear you."

In the sky the planet of love and the planet of war are about to cross one in front of the other, Ash thinks, looking at his astronomer. That is why you came here.

This one time, thinks Qays, I am going to live.

He leans forward and kisses Ash on the mouth.

EIGHT OF COINS

Like a third note in the chord, Nour watches from shore as the two bodies bob in the distance. She sees Ash put his arms around Qays.

The sky's blue seems darker. She looks around savagely. There is no one near her, no one to ask what it is exactly that she is seeing. But this is how it was for her always, she thinks. No one ever needed to ask her for anything because she was always ready.

When her *chand-mumani,* Qays' mother, asked her to go along with Qays to Europe all she had thought about was how much fun it would be to be with Qays alone again, like when they were younger. And since they had come, Qays had been alone in his silence, twitching, still.

Nour made her own light, inventing agendas for them, deciding which museum or neighborhood they might visit.

But I can't give him joy like the sea, she thinks to herself, and then with more clarity. I can't give him joy at all.

What's left inside? she thinks with strange dispassion. What am I left with here on the beach in this strange city in a country whose language I don't speak? After you take away what *chand-mumani* was hoping would happen here, after you take away what her father expected her to do with her life, after you take away her fear at disappointing everyone, even her desperation to feel joy, after you take away all of it, what do you have left? Who is Nour?

Even she in her confusion thinks that what is left might not really be her.

SIX OF CUPS

As the sun sets, Qamar stands in the doorway of Qays' room. She watches the golden beam of sunlight, coloring the whole frame caramel, slowly inch down. Along the frame Mulawwah had marked the boy's heights at their various ages. He hadn't stopped marking their heights even after they were no longer children.

She reaches out and touches his last strange, spidery writing, written only the previous year, "Qays, 65" 22 years old." And above that, "Mikayl, 72" 18 years old."

Neither Mulawwah nor Mikayl nor Qays had ever once mentioned it, but she was dismayed, on her older son's behalf that Mikayl so quickly outgrew him, both taller and broader, though four years younger.

"Our special *bachcha,*" she says out loud to herself. What had Mulawwah meant? Though partly she knew: Qays is so quiet, never very social, not like Mikayl at all, who always seems to have weekend parties to go to and girls calling on the phone for him. "He gets it from you," she tells the open air. "You're the one who was so bookish when we were younger, always studying. I was a healthy normal girl, always outside, always playing sports. My team always won when we played games in school and sometimes even the boys wanted me to play *kabaddi* with them!"

What if it was her then? Who gave Qays his oddness? After all a girl who played sports and cut her hair short like a boy might grow up to be mother of a boy who never fit in. Besides, these days lots of girls play *kabaddi.*

"I made you," she says out loud. "I have every right to look at your things."

She walks inside the room.

SEVEN OF CUPS

The room is in a state of disarray. Qays hasn't put his telescope away. In the big northern window—Qays had chosen his bedroom specifically because it had the best view of the sky—it sits, delicately, the cap carelessly on the table beside it.

Though it isn't yet dark, Qamar bends carefully beside the telescope and looks through the eyepiece. Is that a star? She wants so much to see what he is looking at but doesn't know how to focus the telescope, doesn't know what she is supposed to be seeing, whether the angle of the scope is even right after so many days of Qays being gone.

Sighing, she places the cap back on the lens, carefully so as not to disturb the angle, which may or may not be deliberate.

"Always in my house I am stepping around everything," she says, going over to the nightstand beside Qays' bed. "Why, you must tell me, if I am the head of this house now, should I be so timid?" But the face of Mulawwah in the picture sitting there does not answer.

She sits down on the unmade bed and picks up the thick astronomy book sitting there. It is one from Qays' childhood, one she and Mulawwah had given him on his sixth birthday. Six years old and already obsessed with the sky. Maybe that is all Mulawwah was talking about, she comforts herself, flipping through the book.

Then her breath catches. There is a letter tucked inside. She instantly recognizes Mulawwah's strange handwriting. She always used to tease him that he wrote English script but with Urdu letters. She laughs for a moment but suddenly stops.

The letter is *in* Urdu.

"But Qays doesn't read Urdu. Why would you write to him in Urdu?"

She sees the date—just two days before Mulawwah had died. He must have written it in the hospital. And then, going cold all over her body, she sees the salutation of the letter:

My dear Qamar, my moon-in-the-sky...

NINE OF COINS

Did Nour just see what she thinks she did? The two of them are floating in the water still.

The day around her grows clammy and cold, feels like it is wrapping itself around her, binding her wrists to her sides, wrapping around her stomach. Her chest.

Her throat.

Over the cold gray space between Nour and everyone on the beach around her, a lonely song, a single tune on a guitar. She looks around wildly, trying to see who is playing.

No one is playing.

The blood in her ears beats an accompaniment.

Why can't *I* go in the water? thinks Nour to herself rebelliously, though she already knows the answer, having grown up learning she couldn't even bare her knees and forearms, let alone wear a bathing suit. But why *really,* she wants to know, the slow boil of anger starting to strangle her from the inside the way the coldness of the day smothers her from the outside.

And then she can't breathe. The grains of sand seem to grow in size, the sky flattens out. The waves freeze and the ocean seems like it is only bands of blue and white.

Nour lets out a little moan as she hears the song rising in her ears.

Her sight blurs and she can't make out what is happening between the two in the water.

"Oh no," she says then, and can't stop herself from crying. "No, no, no—"

NINE OF SWORDS

His mouth is on Ash's mouth. He tastes the salt of the ocean on his lips. Ash is melting, enveloping him. The water is warm. The clouds are gathering in the sky above them.

They are two bodies above the water, shivering even though the day is not cold, but below the surface, in the water, their legs entangled, Qays doesn't know where he ends and where Ash begins.

He wants to close his eyes like he's always seen in the soaps, but he also wants to keep looking at Ash's chocolate-brown skin, his coal-black eye lashes, the surface of his lids, trembling, trembling.

He presses his mouth against Ash's lips and then feels Ash's lips yield and open.

"No," says Qays then, pushing Ash away in the water, wiping his own mouth. "No, no, wait."

Ash is looking at him.

"I'm sorry," says Qays. "I didn't mean to so quickly—"

"It's fine," interrupts the other. "I wanted you to—"

"No, but my cousin—" and Qays turns toward the beach, pointing. But Nour doesn't seem to be there.

Ash looks in the direction Qays is pointing.

"Where is she?" he asks. "Where did she go?"

Qays shades his eyes and scans the beach. "I don't know," he says.

TEN OF COINS

Nour is rolling her last shirt into a neat cylinder to put into the
suitcase when Qays bursts into her room at the hostel. "Where
the hell did you go?" he nearly shouts.

"Where's your friend?" asks Nour, primly.

"He's downstairs in the lobby. Why are you packing?"

"Because I am going home," she says, turning her back to him so
she need only control her voice and not her face.

"No, you aren't," he says brusquely, shoving her aside and taking
things out of the suitcase, her jeans, her purple blazer.

"Qays! Qays, stop," she says, but he doesn't listen.

"You were supposed to come with me on this trip, to look at the
planets," he says to himself more than her, distraught.

"Qays *bhai*," she says more tenderly then, laying her hand on
his arm. He stops pulling things out of the suitcase. "Things are
getting confusing, *na?* For you and for me." His shoulders droop.
His chin drops to his chest. He is staring down into her suitcase.

"Don't you want to look at the planets?" he asks plaintively.

"*Bhai-jaan,*" she says quietly, looking over her shoulder through
the open door into the hallway, as if Ash were standing right there.
"It's time to go home."

He looks at her, his face full of sadnesses, all the joy she saw earlier
in the water, drained out.

Her hands feel cold. She feels cold.

She hates herself. She hates herself for hating who he is. She hates herself for having to be the one to say to him what she has to say to him.

TEN OF WANDS

Ashwin stands up when he sees Nour coming down the stairs with her suitcase, walking toward the door, Qays half-running to keep up with her. He can't hear what they are saying, but she is upset, her eyes focused in front of her. He is waving his arms, trying to talk into her face, but she won't look at him.

She looks nowhere but the ground in front of her. Her face is set and it seems as if she has just finished crying and has determined not to cry anymore.

"What happened?" Ash asks loudly, walking towards the two of them.

They pass him.

"I'm sorry if I made you mad," he calls after Nour as she pushes the door of the hotel open and walks out on the street.

Qays looks back at him, his face set and scowling.

"What happened?" asks Ash again, moving closer.

"Don't," says Qays sharply, holding his palms out against the air between them. He turns around and follows Nour onto the street.

Ash walks up to the glass and watches them through it.

Nour is looking out into the street, trying to call the attention of a cab driver, her arm lifted halfway, then dropping, rising again when she sees a headlight. Qays' hand is on her shoulder. She hasn't removed it, but she pays him no attention either. He is talking more quietly now, not trying to get her attention, just talking into her ear.

Slowly her arm drops, and she looks out away from him. From where he stands, Ash can see her face, see her mouth tied shut in sadness, the shining tears trembling with her effort to keep them in her lashes.

TEN OF SWORDS

"Think of your mother, Qays," Nour says softly, still not turning away from the blank sky. Is this why Qays loves the sky? Because by looking at it he doesn't have to look anywhere else?

Qays lets out an anguished sob. "You think I haven't? What am I supposed to do, Nour?"

"Do?" she says sharply, turning around to look at him. "You are supposed to do what you are supposed to do! Be a man. You came here for what reason?"

He is silent, his face gaunt.

"You lied to everyone," she says in the same low tone, like a dull knife. "You lied to me, you lied to your mother. My God, if Mullah-Uncle was alive now, you would have killed him again—"

"Shut up," he says then, fiercely. "You don't know, you don't know—"

"What am *I* supposed to do, Qays?" she wails. "Go home and say what? Say what about what happened here?"

"Don't go then," he says urgently, reaching for her suitcase. "Stay and we can talk about it."

"No," she says, wrenching her suitcase from him and waving for the nearing cab. "No. I am going, final decision. You come and meet me at the airport. Flight is leaving tonight at 11:30 for Zurich and then we switch for New York. We'll be back in Arizona by tomorrow afternoon. Go upstairs and pack."

He does not move.

The cab is at the curb and she is hoisting her suitcase into the back. He is standing at the curb, his mouth in a flat line.

Once inside the cab she tells the driver to take her to the airport. She does not look behind her. She knows Qays is still standing there.

Her shoulders droop and she lets out a long, shuddering breath. She knows he will not come.

EIGHT OF CUPS

The sun has gone down.

Just below the line of the foothills, it casts long orange shadows across the desert, through the cactus garden and into the house.

It streaks across the table, across Qamar's hands, across the letter folded on the table in front of her.

She sits at the table, her mouth half-open, staring at her hands, at the letter folded up between them.

It had taken her five full minutes to reach into the book and lift the letter out of it. She had stood there beside the bed, holding the letter in her hand, staring at the page of the astronomy book for another five minutes. Trying to process the information there. Quasars.

What was a quasar?

She had turned, shuffled from the room into the kitchen, placing one foot in front of the other as if she had never walked through the house before.

She had never walked through this house before, she thought as she had walked, the letter in her hand. Whose house was this?

The paper is old, soft. Mulawwah always wrote with his ballpoint pen so hard onto the surface of the paper that even a new page felt old after he had written on it.

She has been sitting at the table for what seems like hours. Must have been hours, she agrees, since the sun was full in the sky when she sat down, shining through the window in bars, pressing her there, binding her there.

Against the noise in her head, the roar of old and forgotten anger—
how could you leave me?—and the monotone of the white table and
the orange light, she tries to process the information: Mulawwah
had written her a letter, probably on his death bed, or at least
knowing death was soon. Qays had seen the letter. And taken it.

And kept it from her.

For years.

"So you had something to tell me? Something you couldn't say
directly, couldn't say to your own wife? You've been misled, old
man. Your son didn't trust you—"

She stands up violently, the chair falling over. She likes the sound
of it. She wants to knock another chair over.

"You thought I couldn't hear it so you had to write it down. And
he kept you from me."

She drags her knuckles across her eyes. "No. I will not." She takes
the letter up and crumples it in a ball. "What do you have to tell
me, old man, what? *Bolo. Abhi bolo!*"

Silence and the darkening of orange to blue and then black her
only answers.

In the dim light, she feels the crumpled letter in her palm. "What
happens now?" she whispers. "If I read it?"

She opens the letter in the twilight, smooths it out, holds it close
to her face to try to make out the script.

She can see the bare shapes of the letters, but the words themselves
are inscrutable.

NINE OF CUPS

The message light on the phone blinks. Qamar feels something shift inside. There are messages on the phone. She barely remembers turning off the ringer. And so she returns. She folds the letter up and slides it into the pocket of her cardigan. She flicks the kitchen light on and presses the button on the answering machine.

"Qamar *bhabhi*, this is Asad *bhai*. I heard from Nour that everything is going fine in Spain. Not to worry. Our children will be coming home soon to us. Don't be lonely. Call us and come to dinner soon."

"Hello Mrs. Majnoon. This is Mrs. Evelyn. Thank you so much for talking with us this afternoon. We hope we have another chance to talk very soon. Maybe we can come again on Friday?"

"Mama, hey! It's Mikayl! We're having so much fun here! Hope you're not being blue and staying home—see you in a couple of days! Miss you, love you, bye!"

"*Salaam eleikum,* Aunty." Nour's voice sounds quiet, flat. "Things are going very well here, though we are tired from all the traveling." She pauses. "We will see you soon, *inshallah,* soon."

And then Qamar is alone again, alone in the room.

"If Mikayl is home in only a few days, I had better go shopping to get some things," she says, grateful for any distraction. She takes her keys from the hook and her handbag from the counter.

TEN OF CUPS

In front of a bank of peppers, she stops. Rows of them, bright green, orange, yellow, red. She has three cloves of garlic in her hand.

"What's right in front of you, you don't see," she says to the peppers.

Carrots, onions, garlic, peppers, and what? What does she need to make Mikayl's favorite pickle?

She fumbles in her pocket for the paper but what she pulls out is not her hastily scrawled grocery list but the letter.

As the water jets hiss on, spraying the vegetables with a fine mist, she lets out a little whimper, unfolding the crinkled paper.

My dear Qamar, my moon-in-the-sky. I have to tell you a few things and I can't focus on explaining it all. Just hope to tell you and pray to Allah that you will understand what to do on your own if it's His will you do it without me. I think now it may be.

You will have to watch very carefully after our sons. They are susceptible to many influences and while growing up we have been able to shield them but soon they are going to go out into the world and what we have said will be less important than their own lives.

Jaan, Our son Qays is a tender boy, a gift that has been given us. But he is a little different, I think you will notice this as he grows older. I have always seen it, the way he acts and speaks, so gentle and he is always so scared, of what he doesn't say. He needs your guidance always, no matter what. You cannot leave him alone in the world. He is not like Mikayl, he will not be able to manage himself on his own, he needs more support in order to find the right path. If you leave him, he will be lost.

Qamar's throat tightens. She looks up from the letter to the peppers.

From the peppers to the rows of spinach and greens. "Oh, *jaan,* you really shouldn't have left all this to me."

Qays is not like you and me. He has a different path, a difficult one. I can't say why Allah gave him this hardship, or gave him to us, but this is kismet. Do not fail in helping him find his way. You must guide him on the path Allah has given. Remember that everything is God's. Remember me in your prayers. Khudafez. Mulawwah.

FOOL'S ERRAND

2

PAGE OF COINS

In fear, Nour walks down the stairs into the noise- and light-filled terminal, goes to the ticket counter.

Why must she go home if she can go anywhere? Qays was choosing darkness, why can't she choose also?

"I need to change my ticket," she says, sliding it across the counter.

"To where?" the woman asks.

PAGE OF SWORDS

Nour walks.

Down the stairs she walks.

Anywhere she walks.

Anywhere to change she walks.

Walks where.

Noise in the terminal.

Terminal Qays chooses darkness.

Nour choosing what.

Nour walking to want.

Wanting home.

Home to change. Home to fear.

Walking from fear to anywhere.

Nour walking anywhere.

I need to change my ticket.

Qays choosing.

I need to change my ticket says Nour.

Nour walking light.

To where, the woman asks.

To where anywhere.

To want to change to what.

Anywhere where.

Nour walking anywhere.

Filled with could.

Nour chooses light.

PAGE OF WANDS

Something old and cold inside Qays starts rising to the surface.
First his stomach is cold, then his heart and then it blooms on the
surface of his skin like the light frost flowers that appear on the
window in winter.

Wind has carried Nour from him and the night is falling.

"Please explain it to me," says Ash but now Qays is deaf, strangled
by absence—of Nour, of his father, of the sun in the sky.

Is this why he has always loved planets, because they are cold and
lonely, alone in expanses of space with no one near?

"Why did your cousin leave?" Ash asks again and even though Qays
knows all the reasons, knows how stupid they are, how small, he
is flushed full of shame.

Shame that Nour left him, shame that she was right to do so.

Shame for all the years of silence he turned his back on his own
heart even when he prayed his father had meant in that letter what
he thought he had meant.

Shame for hiding the letter from his mother, for keeping silent, for
letting all the long years pass between them without ever believing
what he had always been taught: that a mother loves her son with
no condition or limit.

Shame he had not been able to be brave enough to have faith.

He's betrayed everyone, he realizes with a sickening start. Betrayed
Nour by bringing her on this trip, betrayed his father by taking
his letter, betrayed his mother by not trusting her.

Even Ash, who believes his feelings are uncomplicated—he is going to betray Ash as well, betray him by cutting things off, by not saying anything about why, by going home, by refusing to even look at what he feels right now, this very minute.

PAGE OF CUPS

"Qays," Ash says tenderly, taking his hands, sitting down on the bench next to him.

The street is wild and cold around them.

Qays feels how Ash must feel all the time: the sounds of the street, the traffic, the people, everything is muted. All he can hear is his own breathing, his own heart and faintly somewhere in the background, his father's voice reciting evening prayers.

His father with that soft voice of his, soft and fearsome.

"Qays."

Qays likes the way Ash says his name, muted, blurred, more of an animal sound. He can't manage the throaty 'q' or the dipthong. He says "Kess," the way Nour used to say his name when they were little.

Ash's hands are holding his hands. Ash speaks with his hands, Qays thinks. If he is holding someone's hands then he can't speak to them. He has to say everything with touch.

Smell of rosemary in the air, the street twists down out of sight.

Ash holds his right hand but one of his fingers is stroking Qays' palm.

"I used to really believe you could read a fortune in someone's hand," Qays says. "Until someone read my palm and said I would only have one serious love in my life and it would be at the beginning when I was very young and that I wouldn't love again after that."

"So who was your one serious love?" Ash asks him.

"I think it was my father," Qays says, covering his face with his hands to hold in the sob he feels gathering in his gut.

KNIGHT OF COINS

Nour gets off the plane in New York and doesn't get on her connecting flight. She fetches her suitcase from the overhead bin, catches the bus straight to 8th Avenue and gets off, dragging her bag on its little wheels out of the terminal and onto the sidewalk.

You can't see any stars from here, she thinks, feeling grateful. So now what? I can't go back and I can't home because if I go home I will have to start answering questions and I don't know how to answer them.

The light changes and without thinking too much about where she is going, Nour crosses the street.

It feels like the first time, she thinks, that she has been alone. "Alone!" she says out loud and it is funny to her because she is surrounded by hundreds of people all walking toward and away from her at once. She's never been more crowded yet it is just her, no aunty, no father, no Qays, just Nour in the middle of the world.

Is this what Qays felt in the ocean, far from shore, finally willing to open himself to something?

And then somehow, strangely, she remembers: Qays' oddities, his moods, his loneliness. Is this the reason why?

"So why do I get stuck with explaining it?" she wants to know, plaintively. The light at Seventh Avenue is red. She has to wait. She sees ahead of her a great glow of red, purple, blue—she is amazed. "What *is* that?" she asks a man standing next to her, also waiting for the light, an orange umbrella under his arm though the sky is clear.

"First time in New York?" he asks her and even though she nods, he doesn't say anything else, leaves her at the curb walking quickly away when the light changes.

She hurries forward, toward the lights—they are marquees, advertisements, news-crawls running on the sides of the buildings. It's Times Square, she realizes. Nothing in the news-crawls about the planetary confluence, she notices.

Is every surface written on, she wonders, realizing then that even she wrote scripture and judgment on the surface of the sea on the skin of Qays' body.

She closes her eyes in despair remembering the look of sweet joy on his face, the happiness—she had never seen him look like that before and her first reaction had been anger.

She opens her eyes. They are full of tears, wishing she could see Qays, talk to him and then—*there*—across the street—he is.

KNIGHT OF WANDS

"Do you have to go home?" Ash asks him, still stroking his palm.

Qays turns to look at him. "Not yet," he says and then leans over and kisses Ash on the mouth. "Make me forget," he whispers into Ash's ear, knowing that Ash cannot hear him. "Kiss me and make me forget about them. Kiss me then kill me so I never have to leave you, never have to lose you, never have to go home again."

Because Qays knows that Ash can't hear him, can only feel Qays' lips moving against his ear, Qays keeps whispering.

"I want to stay here and find out if I can love you. I want to forget everything that I was taught. I don't want a father and mother anymore. I only want you, what you can give me, what you can teach me, what you know about me that no one else knows about me. I want my body to feel the way it feels when you touch me."

Mistaking panic for passion, Ash twists free and kisses Qays deeply, holding both of Qays' ears in his hands.

Qays feels himself disappear minute by minute.

He wants to be crushed by time, drowned in this minute. He wants never to have to resurface, to never have to answer Ash, never to have to leave him, never have to explain.

KNIGHT OF SWORDS

She blinks for a minute, seeing him, across the street, wearing black, talking to someone else who is occluded by the crowd. Qays in New York? He's laughing. She likes the smile on his face. How did he get here before her?

What can she say to him now? She only has a minute to rehearse it. The cars rush by, the light is still red.

"I don't understand it, Qays," she says out loud. "And also it makes me angry. You threw everything off so easily, all the things you were taught—that *we* were taught."

Nour finds herself feeling jealous. Jealous that he can kiss a man, so easily ignore all the things she let kill herself so sweetly while growing up. All the reasons she was supposed to be a "good girl," not be too loud, not go away to school, not to wear certain clothes, not to behave a certain way—

She fixes on his face. He hasn't noticed her. His hair blows a little in the wind. He seems so carefree, so relaxed. His face is open and clear, not pinched like usual. He is loose, casual. How had she not noticed that before? Could he really have changed so much in just a day? What happened after she left?

The light changes and people begin crossing the street. She stays where she is, rooted to the sidewalk. She can catch short glimpses of him walking across the street toward her.

She wants to forgive him. She wants to tell him what it means to her that he is following his own path in life.

He moves with long, easy strides. Now she can see him more clearly, with his friend, another young man beside him. Shining in the evening light. Now she sees.

It's not him. Not Qays. Not the dark brother. The other one.

Mikayl.

KNIGHT OF CUPS

They walk all night long and Qays whispers all night long. They do not let go of each others' hands, Ash because he realizes he can trace Spanish words into Qays' palm without him understanding them and Qays because he knows that when he lets go of Ash's hand it will be forever.

"Why are you so sad?" Ash traces into the palm of Qays' hand. "Your mother will love you. And your cousin too. I think you just surprised her a little bit. I think she had a plan of her own for a little while."

"What you must think of me," Qays whispers in the dark, knowing Ash can't hear him. "That I am a fool and a child and an idiot that I can't even face you, can't even look at you." He squeezes Ash's hand even tighter but Ash loosens his grip and starts stroking his palm with his fingers. Is he spelling something? Qays can't tell.

"When you hold me too tightly I can't speak to you," Ash traces onto Qays' palm. "You are beautiful with your big scared eyes and little, little mouth. You are a little mouse. My little mouse. Don't go home yet. Stay for a little while. How are we supposed to know anything unless you stay for a little while?"

"I have to go and look at the sky and then I have to leave you and go home," whispers Qays. "If I stay I will just leave you sooner. I would rather love you as much as I can and leave fast."

"How will I be able to keep you?" Ash wonders on Qays' skin. "Let me tell the ending of this story another way."

And while Qays looks longingly up at the black expanse, Ash turns his palm flat up and begins drawing a new fortune there.

QUEEN OF WANDS

The next afternoon Qays sits alone in the garden of the hermitage behind the Sagrat Cor on the highest ridge of Mount Tibidabo. He has come early so he can spend some time checking the star charts and his compass so he can position the telescope properly to catch the right angle of the night sky.

As orange turns to blue then black the sky opens like loose pages, an unbound book, lines and words launching into space like the night-birds that arrow screaming from the rocks over the light net of the city below.

It was odd, positioning the scope to look at what seemed to be brilliant and opaque blue but which in only a few hours would be black endlessness.

When he first arrived off the funicular car he worried about finding a place far enough away from the lights and sounds of the cathedral, the restaurant, the amusement park. He followed a little path along the ridge and soon came to the small hermitage he hadn't even known about.

He waited there then, waited as the light changed.

THE MAGICIAN

To see the light in the sky, why.

He wants proof, proof that pages of equations, weeks of studying the physics of orbital trajectories and the way light bends really did manifest themselves in the physical world.

If math can add up the edges of the rock, if the way planets swing around the sun in the sky can be plotted, then he is sure there is an explanation for himself.

THE HIGH PRIESTESS

Qamar folds the note back up.

The well-creased note.

He must have opened it many times to read it to himself.

"So, Mulawwah, once again you knew what no one knew."

The hissing sound of the water jets comes on, sprays the vegetables, turns off.

Still she stands there, the letter in her hands, in the produce section.

What does it mean? She wants to know, but there is no one, not Mulawwah, not the missionary women, not God, no one to answer her.

THE EMPRESS

And then, as if by thinking of her she called her into being, she sees one of the women, Mrs. Miriam, further down the aisle of the store, pushing a shopping cart.

What does she have in there? Spaghetti squash, broccoli, some salad dressing.

The woman is just in front of her, looking at potatoes, the yellow ones and the brown ones.

"These ones are better for mashing," says Qamar suddenly, pointing at the brown potatoes, "and these ones are better for frying."

"Oh hello dear!" says Mrs. Miriam, recognizing Qamar.

"My son is gone," blurts out Qamar. "Gone to Europe to look at the sky. And I don't know who he is anymore, don't know if he still loves me."

Mrs. Miriam stares, surprised.

"I ... I think he has forgotten what we tried to teach him," Qamar stammers. "I think he lost his way."

Mrs. Miriam smiles, chooses four brown potatoes. "Maybe," she says slowly, like she is still thinking about it, "you should go out and look at the sky as well."

THE EMPEROR

To the naked eye, the planets, the one in front and the one behind, seem just as bright as a star. You cannot even tell there is a shadow inside, cannot tell there is a second whole world inside.

Not really inside, really in front of, really visible there all along.

And not even a shadow—the sun's light is hitting both at once, and they are not occluding each other but shining in the sky very close, so close as to appear as one.

Planet of love, planet of war, thinks Qays, his eye against the eye-piece, his heart filling with years in Ash's arms, years at home, alone in his room, years of silence between him and his mother, years of conversations that avoid the center, avoid the planet that spins around them, the second planet, the one no one wants to see.

And in the case of Venus and Mars, two planets more than just opposite—Venus full of storms and clouds and Mars wiped bare and barren, baring marks of some past, ancient life, long since disappeared.

He remembers then the day they buried his father. He left the mosque and was standing in the parking lot, looking up at the blue sky. Inside the men were chanting chapters and the women, in their separate room, were keening. Between the chanting and the keening, he felt like the lid of his life was being unscrewed. Suddenly the blue sky seemed transparent, that he could look up and see the black void.

My father's body held me in this world, Qays thought then. And now that he is gone, I am no longer anchored to this planet. And even the day is night.

THE HIGH PRIEST

Like a heavenly body he moves across the street toward her, his eyes catching hers but not registering her. They flick back to his friend and then back at her with a flash.

"Nour!" he says in shock, recognizing her now as he steps onto the curb. "Nour, what are you doing in New York? You're supposed to be with Qays! Joseph, it's my cousin, Nour!"

She smiles and gives him a quick hug, as light a touch as is appropriate and then nods at his friend, keeping her hands at her sides as she was taught.

"I left early," she says, trying to sound casual. "Qays is so boring, always going on and on about the stars," she pouts.

"Yeah, that is big brother," he agrees neutrally, keeping his eyes on her.

He doesn't believe her, she realizes. "So I came into the city," she says. "I had such a long time between my flights."

"I am flying home tonight as well," he says. "Maybe we can switch to be on the same plane?"

Oh dear, she thinks, her stomach sinking. Now I will have to explain. Which means I will have to lie.

QUEEN OF SWORDS

Qamar closes the back door of the house and walks out onto the patio. The desert night is cold in February, quite cold. Her shawl is wrapped around her, one of Qays' old telescopes in her left hand, the tripod for mounting it in her right.

Ash walks through the doors of Santa Maria del Mar. The church is empty. There are forty microphones set up in a circle around the floor. An art installation called "Motet."

I have never put my hope in any other than You

She walks from the house, picking her way through ice plants, hoping there aren't snakes in the ground. She keeps her eyes on the fading light behind the foothills off in the distance.

He passes each speaker feeling the vibration on his skin, in his bones, but lightly, very lightly. He hears the music as a rumble or a mumble, something that exists always and eternally in the background.

God of Israel who shows both anger and grace

At a certain place where the light of the house is just a little prick of flame behind her and the sun behind the hills is bluer and beginning to blur with the rocks, she pitches the tripod down and fumbled to fit the scope onto it.

He wants to go back into the water with Qays, so their bodies can touch. Just so he can feel a little tenderness for a little while longer. Is there a sound to the universe like Qays was trying to tell him? And if there was, what did it sound like? Would Ash be able to hear it? Or feel it on his skin?

And who diminishes and disappears all the tribulations of those that suffer

She angles the telescope skyward. She doesn't know what to look for or what she is looking at. When she looks through the eyepiece all she sees is darkness.

Anyhow, thinks Ash, as he sits on the ground in the middle of the forty speakers, each speaking a line of the poem simultaneously, he is not aware of cacophony or background noise. He can only hear one thing at a time. So if the universe is really making sound it hardly matters.

Lord God creator of the sky and the ground remember us how small we are how unknowing

QUEEN OF COINS

"We have to get our check soon and leave to catch the plane," says Mikayl. They are sitting at a café counter. Nour keeps turning to look and make sure her suitcase is still beside her. "No one is going to take it, Nour," Mikayl says.

"You know the city has a kind of music," Nour says.

He smiles. "The cars, the traffic, the racket…"

"I more mean the human voices. I mean just close your eyes and sit for a minute. A real minute. An actual minute." She takes her watch off and puts it on the counter in front of them. "Now, just listen to it." She purses her lips and fixes her gaze on the watch.

He is looking at her but also silent.

In the time that passes, and to Mikayl it seems nearly endless time, he can hear everyone in the café, nearly at once, just a blanket of strange sound, but also individually: he can hear conversations three tables over, he can hear the kitchen workers talking through the service window, he can hear the waitress taking an order, a woman talking on her phone as she comes through the door.

"It's amazing," he admits.

"Mikayl," she chides, "that was only ten seconds."

"Really?"

"Really."

"No."

"A minute is a long time when you are just listening. That's what music is to me."

"I bet Uncle flipped his lid when you changed your major."

"I didn't tell him yet," says Nour. "But it is not as if I am betraying his foundational beliefs," she mutters as an afterthought.

"You just might be," Mikayl says, smiling.

"I wish my father was more like Qamar Aunty," Nour says. "She never minded when you wanted to study art or that Qays spends all his time looking at the sky."

"Well, I think she was just glad Qays was passionate about something. And as for me..." His look turns inward though his gaze drifts out toward the street. "As for me, I think she was just glad I wasn't turning out like Qays."

THE LOVERS

"Like Qays?" Nour asks, trying to sound as if she had no idea what he means. "What do you mean?"

He looks at Nour and puts down his coffee cup. "Why did you come home, Nour? What happened in Spain?"

"I told you," she says, fidgeting, gesturing the waitress over. "I was bored. I wanted to go and see things and Qays is forever looking upward. At nothing."

The waitress comes and puts the check down.

"Yeah," says Mikayl, as if Nour had somehow just admitted everything. "I always wonder when he is going to give that up and look at himself. I keep waiting…"

"Waiting? Why would you want that?"

He looks at her with, it seems, pity. "Don't you see how different he is now? How unsure, how unlike himself? Don't you *miss* Qays the way he used to be when we were all kids? Don't you remember how crazy he was, all those tricks he would play, how much he *laughed*?"

She blinks. She remembers Qays as a tender and sometimes silly little boy. He *had* been a jokester, but had he really changed that much?

"Don't you *want* him to find his way out of whatever sadness he is stuck in?"

"It's because ever since Mulawwah-Uncle died—"

"No," interrupts Mikayl. "That's not why."

Qays? Sad? *Sad?* She had never even thought—

"Come on," he says, losing his patience. He stands and puts some money down on the counter. "We have to hurry if we are going to make the plane."

THE CHARIOT

Mikayl hefts her suitcase into the trunk of the cab.

"Why would Qamar Aunty be happy that you didn't turn out to be like Qays?" she asks him. "That's not a very nice thing to say."

They get into the back of the cab. "We are going to the Newark airport," Mikayl tells the driver. For a moment, Nour notices how even though she is older and has been traveling on her own, it is easy for Mikayl take charge of them.

The cab joins the train of traffic heading for the tunnel.

"He is smart, he studies hard, he never got into trouble."

"Unlike me, you mean," says Mikayl.

"Well there was that time Aunty found the beer bottles hidden in your bedroom closet."

"At least they weren't open yet."

"So you drinking alcohol is somehow better in a way than Qays—"

"I don't think it is better or worse, just different. Very, very different."

"How different?"

"Well with me she could take the bottles away, make me swear never to drink again, threaten me, smack me—"

"Qamar Aunty would never hit you!" she says, with indignation on her aunt's behalf.

"Wouldn't she?" he scoffs with a guilty smile. "Anyhow, that situation is easy more or less. With Qays…"

"With Qays what?" she asks. How can he say that about Qamar Aunty? And is that what she had done to Qays in Europe? Somehow in some way actually *hit* him?

"How do you change the waters of the ocean, Nour? Or the space in the sky? You might not understand it but some things just *are*. That's why people get so angry. Because they know somewhere inside that they are just *wrong*. That maybe what they've been taught about God and prophets and other things their whole life is just *wrong*."

She turns from Mikayl to look out the window. They enter the tunnel. There is nothing to look at so she looks at her reflection in the black glass. She imagines she can feel the river moving above them.

STRENGTH

Her reflection looks back.

In her music class they were studying the form of the motet—
multiple voices at once, usually composed for five separate choirs
of eight voices each.

Forty voices singing at once in different registers, poems that
thicken in the air itself.

She hears the music of the tires on the road, the cars before and
behind, the sound of the driver's radio, the little television in the
back seat, Mikayl's finger's drumming the armrest, her breathing
in her ear.

Why hadn't she paid closer attention when Qays told her the
universe had a sound? Because if the universe has a sound then
she would make a sound that would be a part of it. And what is
that sound?

She can't get the look on Qays' face out of her mind.

The look on his face in the ocean: joy.

The look on his face on the street when she left him: crumpling,
closing in, the dying of light at the end of the day.

She looks down at her hands.

What note will she play?

THE HERMIT

He looks. He takes notes. He looks again.

The sky is clear, has been clear.

If he is grateful to God, he is grateful to the wind, the wind that comes over the sea—what is it called, a zephyr? A mistral?

Wind in an endless series of pathways and influences that spread across the planet, encircle it. Encircle me. My mother's hands.

He lies back on the stone wall and closes his eyes and dreams of his mother.

There is no moon in the sky tonight, he knows, and a good thing too, nothing would have been visible had the bright sunned moon been shining.

He turns his face in the direction of the wind and closes his eyes. The cold wind on his skin causes tears to seep out. Zephyr. From the Arabic word "zeffer."

The silence has a fullness and he thinks of Ash, down in Santa Maria del Mar, listening to the music of the forty voices.

Even deaf, he hears.

THE WHEEL OF FORTUNE

And so what do I do now?

Nothing: he will leave soon or he will stay. But it doesn't have anything to do with me. He is listening to something inside.

He is listening to God.

Or listening to fear.

What I do next—what is it, just one person making a single sound against what must be the entire universe resounding?

Could you see a single star in the sky moving?

Of course: a shooting star, arrowing across the sky.

But a shooting star isn't really moving. It's falling.

Should I speak at all?

Should I reach for him?

Or do I just wait, see which way he drifts on his own? Toward me or farther away, away out into space.

And is this how the moon feels, with no light of its own at all, spinning and wheeling endlessly through space, not shining, only shone upon?

Qays, crazy star-gazer, come down from the mountain.

Come down from the sky and find me.

QUEEN OF CUPS

Qamar looks up again at the sky. Near the horizon a very bright star. If she remembers correctly, it is Venus, not a star but a planet and close.

She can hear Qays at eight years old, explaining it to her in perfect seriousness: "Mama, see it doesn't twinkle like a star it's solid and a little blue, can you tell?"

"Yes, I can see the blue," she had said even though she hadn't.

But she sees it now, thick, bright, constant. She tries to adjust the telescope in the direction of the planet. She looks through the eyepiece. Blackness. She shifts the telescope again. She looks again.

"Oh, I'm going to find you," she croons to herself, her hands now on the body of the telescope itself, her eye still at the lens, shifting it bit by tiny bit. "I'm going to find you."

She looks up for a minute at the sky, fighting frustration. It's right *there*. Why can't she find it in the telescope?

"Because Ma," she hears Qays saying in her ear, "the sky is infinite. You're looking for one prick of light in all of space. Like a needle in a haystack."

"Needle in a haystack, I can find," she says flatly. "Or a letter in a book I am not supposed to see."

She bends back to the lens, her hands once again on the scope. She stabs the telescope blindly at the sky, first here then there.

"How *could* you?" she says, but almost immediately is unsure whom she is accusing. And of what.

JUSTICE

Ash emerges from the church, dizzy because for him, leaving the closed space with its resounding echoes and entering the street is a reverse motion in sound.

Everything recedes from him and he is plunged into a blanketed, muted silence.

He feels like he is coming out of the ocean, the silty water washing from him.

Qays will be up at the observatory for most of the night, he thinks. He can leave him there and go wait at his hotel.

Or maybe he should just go home.

THE HANGED MAN

"You stay in the sky," she says to God, "and you, dear husband, stay in the earth. And my son, maybe he should stay wherever he has gone too. Maybe that is best."

And then, by accident, by odd equation of her frenzied swings, something comes into view of the telescope.

It's not enormous—but it is something she's looking at: the size of a big marble perhaps, or a silver dollar, blue and white.

"But it looks like the earth," she says out loud. "Same-same as the earth."

She gazes then, transfixed, for long minutes at the sky. Does she just imagine the clouds swirling lazily across its surface? Is that motion on the surface of the planet itself or is it inside her own eyes?

Or somewhere in the infinite space in between.

The blue calm surface of Venus, she's found it.

But I know the truth of you, she says. She remembers because Qays explained it to her.

"Stay still there," she begs the planet. "Stay there all night. Don't move. Let me just look at you."

But she knows the planet is moving and for that matter so is she, standing on the surface of the Earth, being spun slowly away.

DEATH

She leaves the telescope where it is, in the middle of the field behind the house and begins walking slowly back. It feels chillier. Every once in a while she turns around and casts a look back at the bright spot she knows now to be Venus, slowly rising higher and higher in the sky.

Once in a while, so surrounded by other stars, she forgets which one it is.

She comes close to the house, lit from inside, but avoids it, walking to the side and around to the front porch. Though she is wearing just a *shalwar-kameez* and a shawl, she sits down on the porch, gazing out at the driveway and front lawn.

She's not thinking about it, she's barely even paying attention, staring straight ahead not even at the road but at the mailbox, the green bristles of grass, the concrete curb. She looks at the doors of all the other houses on the street, one by one in a row.

What is it like, she wonders, to be like the women who came to her house the other day, knocking on peoples' doors, going inside, speaking to them because you knew your life was the way these people should be living theirs, that what you believed was so good that you knew you had a responsibility to share with everyone else so they could learn to believe the same things?

Qamar laughs. She laughs and then she cries for just a moment, lifting her shawl to her eyes and blotting the tears away.

"It's *my* house," she says to herself, leaning back against the door. "*I* own this house. Everything in it belongs to *me*. All of the riches there and all the difficult things and sorrows too. Mine."

KING OF COINS

Overhead she sees only flat gray. Here in the front yard you cannot see any stars, she realizes. The street lamps don't look so bright.

It's a lonely street and it is late at night so she is surprised to see a car coming down the road. The headlights stop just short of her driveway. It's a taxi cab.

With her hands on her knees she pushes herself up to standing. "Who is it?" she calls out.

"Mama!" calls Mikayl from the driveway. "Mama, do you have any cash? We need seven more dollars!"

Covered in the blanket of her relief, she pushes aside the stars, the cold empty sky and hurries down the driveway to embrace her son. "Why you didn't tell me you were coming, son? How come so late at night as well? Did you change your plane? I thought you were coming tomorrow only."

Another figure steps from around the cab, a suitcase in her hand.

"Hello, Aunty," says Nour.

TEMPERANCE

"What?" says her aunt weakly. In confusion. "What—what is this?"

Nour looks to Mikayl for assistance, but he has hefted his bag over his shoulder and is heading for the house.

"Aunty, I..."

"You've come home early, *behti*—why? Where is Qays? You left him there?" Her voice is rising.

Nour feels pressed back by her, but pressed back against what? The cab is gone, there's nothing behind her but the street.

"I wanted to come home," she looks down at her hands. She tries not to cry. "Everything seemed like it was changing..."

"Who was changing?" her aunt asks. "Who? Qays? What did he say? What did he do?"

"No," Nour says, raising her hand up. "Not him. Me. I was changing. I changed."

Qamar Aunty stares at her. The light of the street lamp casts dark shadows on her face.

"I can't take care of Qays for you anymore, Aunty," she says then, wiping her hand across her face. "He has to take care of himself."

"He *can't* take care of himself!" Qamar Aunty nearly shouts, pulling a piece of folded up paper from her pocket and waving it in Nour's face. "He *can't*. Everyone knows that. *You* know that."

"Not anymore," says Nour slowly. She looks up at the sky then, expecting to see—what? She doesn't know. But she knows with certainty that the sky is full. If only she could find a place dark enough spot to watch, she knows she would see *something*.

Her aunt is looking down at the letter, reading it, her lips moving slightly as in prayer.

"Aunty, is Qays' telescope still here?"

"His telescope?" she looks up in confusion. "For what?"

Nour looks up at the sky again, shading her eyes against the street lamps. "It's time."

THE DEVIL

It was the devil that came here to speak to him, Qays thinks to himself at the blackest part of the night. He lies down along the stone wall, his hands behind his head as a pillow.

The dead of the night, they call it. Dead because nothing moves.

"But you move," he says to the stars. "You move endlessly, eternally without cease."

So who do you belong to? the night asks him back. To your own body, to the stars in the sky, to the earth, to your mother, to God?

Qays stares up at the sky. Even without the telescope, here in such a dark night, he can see movements. Very occasionally the streak of a shooting star.

The night is a thick, alive, breathing thing that comes down against him, spilling into every opening, snaking under his shirt, against his skin.

His favorite things to search for are the slow, steady circles of satellites, usually moving against the grain of the horizon but not always.

You can't love them so much, says the blackness with reproach. Ugly things, nothing but machines.

"But what am I," asks Qays, "but a machine? If all I am is something that belongs to something else."

What else could you be? the night whispers. Or haven't you understood anything?

"What if," he pauses, "what if I belonged to Ash?"

The night gathers itself in fury.

"Or what if I belonged to myself?"

As soon as he says it he feels the night pull back, pull back from his body, pull straight up into the sky, harden into a black dome above him, the sky no longer full, the stars no longer pulsating in space, all motion still.

Qays props himself up on his elbows. Is that something he heard? But there's only silence.

THE TOWER

Having seen what he had climbed the mountain to see, Qays finds himself no wiser. His hands feel numb as he detaches the eyepiece, begins to pack the telescope back into its case.

When the sky stopped speaking to him, he listened harder. Is this what it is like, to own yourself? he wonders in sadness. To just float on the surface of the world? To be your own boat, to never know anything else?

He hefts the scope on his shoulder and heads down the little path that snakes around the church leading to the overgrown garden that shields it from the road.

The black sky has just started to turn midnight blue and birds and other creatures rustle in the brush.

There's no funicular at this hour, nor taxi, nor person abroad.

Qays begins the long walk down the mountain back to the city which even now is brightly lit against the darkness.

The road ahead of him isn't lit, but by starlight and hours of darkness vision, he can make his way through the black and gray world.

There is a shape on the road ahead of him. A rock? A creature? It moves.

"Qays?" asks Ash.

Qays smiles in the darkness.

"Qays, is it you?"

Qays comes closer, puts the scope gingerly down. He takes Ash's hands in his. He puts Ash's cold hands under his shirt, against his warm skin. He winces just a little bit when they first touch.

"It's you," Ash says.

As the stars in the sky hold their breath, Qays takes Ash's ears in his soft hands.

"Now I can hear the ocean in your hands," says Ash.

Qays kisses him and the sky washes ashore.

KING OF SWORDS

Qamar had left Nour at the telescope, peering up at the darkness where Venus had been a moment before, and come back to the house to find Mikayl in his room, the door closed.

The guest bedroom beckons but with Mikayl home, she knows Nour will also need a place to sleep for the night before heading to her own home the next day. Now that she has laid eyes on a planet, Qamar feels braver, less wary of the large, empty bed. She walks straight in without looking to the side at the open door of the guest room.

"What do I owe you?" she asks the empty room as she passes it and closes the door to her own bedroom, lies down in the bed for the first time in what seems like ages and closes her eyes.

The night is sharp against her skin. It cramps her so she feels like she cannot move. As if by an inconsiderate bedmate, she feels pressed against the edge of the bed. Pressed by nothing but empty space, she thinks to herself. Pressed but by nothing.

Every time she feels herself settling down into half-sleep, one of the sharp knives of night's edge draws against her skin and wakes her, reminding her of the endless space night makes outside, in the fields and streets, and the endless absence that death brings inside, into the house, into the heart.

THE STAR

They sit on a rock near the lower promontory and watch the light from the sun rising behind them spread across the city. When it reaches the base of Montjuic, Ash rests his head on Qays' shoulder.

"I can't believe I have known you for such a short time," says Qays.

Ash springs up when he feels the vibrations of voice rushing through Qays' body. "What did you say?" he asks.

"I said it's funny that I only met just you."

Ash leans over and nuzzles Qays' neck, kissing him and nibbling a little. Qays laughs and pulls him up to look in his face.

"Do you feel like that too?" he asks.

"Yes," says Ash. "I don't want you to go home. Stay one more week."

Qays looks down at the city. "I can't. I have to go home."

"Why do you have to go home?" asks Ash. "They don't understand you there. I want you to stay. We hardly got to know each other. We haven't had enough time."

"What if I promised to come back? Will you still be here?"

Ash searches Qays' eyes for some oracle of intent but sees nothing there but the question.

THE MOON

Qamar opens her eyes. The room is brightly lit. She cannot remember having slept at all. It seems to her like the devil night was howling at her until sunrise.

"*Ya Allah,*" she says pushing herself awake and wrapping a shawl around her night dress.

She hears sounds outside the room. Mikayl must be awake. She opens the door and there he is, his back to her, standing in front of the marked door frame, touching the height measurement. He senses her and turns around and gives her a big smile.

"Hi Mama," he says and kisses her on the cheek.

"You boys grew up so fast," she says.

"Yeah but is Qays *really* this short?" he asks, pointing at the last marker.

She laughs and chucks him gently on the back of his head. "Don't talk with such disrespect about your elder brother. Do you know what would happen to us if we talked with disrespect about our elder brothers, sisters and cousins?"

"Oh here we go," says Mikayl, heading down the hall to the kitchen.

"We would get beaten!" she says, chopping the air with her hand as she followed him.

"Yes I seem to remember a couple of swats with the old wooden spoon myself," he says, putting the kettle on the stove for tea.

"Yes," she says, "and you'll get a couple more if you keep up like this."

"But you would never hit Qays," he says.

She sniffs. "Qays never misbehaved. Not like you. Qays is different."

"How different, Mama?" he asks, leaning on the counter with his elbows so he can look her straight in the eye. "How do you think Qays is different from me?"

She looks away from him, out at the desert, the hills beyond. "I left his telescope out in the yard," she says, remembering.

THE SUN

They pick their way through the ice plants in the backyard and into the scrubby expanse that borders the expanse stretching to the hills.

"Mama, you walked all the way out here?"

"I wanted to get away from the lights of the street and the house so I could see the sky."

"Now you sound just like him."

She laughs. "Do you know we gave him his first astronomy books when he was only six? And he read them even if he had no idea what was inside."

"Something sunk in," says Mikayl.

Where is the scope, Qamar wonders. She doesn't see it ahead. "Maybe we went another way?"

"No, there!" calls Mikayl pointing at something on the ground.

"Oh my God!" she shouts and starts running.

Curled up on the ground, her head resting on the telescope case, her jacket thrown over her body, is Nour.

"Nour, *ya Allah*, what are you doing here in the wilderness?" Qamar says, crouching down and putting her hands on the girl's shivering body.

"Oh Aunty," Nour murmurs, "I think I fell asleep in the sky."

"*Batameez!*" scolds Qamar. "You could have frozen to death or been devoured by some wolf!"

"Mama, there are no wolves in Arizona."

"You shut up," she says. "You don't know that! And there are coyotes. And jackals. And snakes. And worse things!"

"Oh but the sky was so beautiful," says Nour. "How could you bear to go back inside under the flat ceiling? How could you leave it…"

"Now you are mad too," she says in disgust, rising up. "Come, come quickly back to the house and have a hot shower."

Mikayl helps Nour, still drowsy, to stand. She leans on him heavily as they walk towards the house, Qamar following a little distance behind, the case on her shoulder and the telescope with tripod still attached in her arms.

"Oh Mikayl," mutters Nour, still trying to fully wake, "the sun is so strong, I can't believe it didn't wake me up."

"You must be freezing," he says.

"I could hardly sleep all night," she admits, "and the night is really loud."

KING OF WANDS

When Mikayl comes into the kitchen, Qamar is preparing breakfast. He can tell by the way she is banging the pots and pans and slamming the lids that they are in for it.

Only after Qamar hears the sound of water rushing in the shower does she calm down.

"Mom, chill a little bit," says Mikayl coming into the kitchen.

"Chill? That's your answer? It was *dangerous,* Mikayl! To be out all night. For a *girl.*"

"Stop it, Mama. Listen to yourself!"

"No, *you* listen!" she shouts, throwing the pan in her hand down on the stove. "Don't defend her! Don't think all this foolishness doesn't matter! Coming home early from a trip and in the middle of the night. Wandering off into the desert with all these stupid ideas. Where did it get her? Where does it get you?"

He is silent.

"You think I don't understand what is happening?" she shouts again, coming close, just inches from his face. "Say something! Say something to me!"

"I don't know what you want, Mommy," he says softly.

"If your father were here," she begins.

"But he's not," snaps Mikayl. "And if he was, Mama, he wouldn't care. Don't you understand that? He wouldn't care!"

She looks at him for a moment, her face completely panicked. And then slaps him across the face.

"Mom!" he cries out holding his cheek.

She grabs his ear with one hand and slaps him again with the other. "No, he *isn't* here! I am here. And I am telling you what you and your brother and your cousin don't know: you listen to us and what we taught you. We know better than you do."

She tries to slap him again but he slips out, wiggles away from her and goes to the other side of the counter. "You can't do this, Mom," he says, crying and shouting at the same time.

In the silence that has settled in the kitchen she realizes the water has stopped. Nour is standing in the hallway, a towel around her body, curls hanging damp around her shoulders.

"Oh *behti,*" she says, forcing sweetness into her shaking voice. "Do you want some fried eggs?"

"Aunty, it's not Mikayl's fault. Or Qays," she says. "I didn't leave Qays because I wanted something he couldn't give me. I left because I realized there is nothing I wanted. Now I have to learn about what I want."

"Foolishness," Qamar snaps. "Everyone has gone crazy!"

And she brushes past Nour, grabbing the key to her car from the hook by the garage door and slams out of the house, the screen door banging behind her.

She drives halfway down the block before she remembers she left the stove on. For a moment she considers going back but realizes she doesn't care.

JUDGMENT

Qamar drives.

She has no plan or destination.

The wind blows through the open windows onto her hot skin.

She is still shaking from striking Mikayl.

Is it true that she has never struck Qays?

"Because he is my best little boy," she says with a sob and tears fill her eyes, blurring her vision. She pulls over to the side of the road quickly and collapses over the steering wheel, her stomach heaving. "Qays, my *bachcha,* come home now," she pleads into the wheel. She presses her forehead into its rubber edge to calm herself down.

She tries to picture the serene surface of the blue planet in the sky, the white clouds hanging there.

She looks up over the rim of the dashboard like it was the horizon and then realizes where she is. The *qabarstaan.*

Still wearing her night dress she walks through the green alleys to the flat stone set into the earth with Mulawwah's name on it.

From her pocket she pulls the letter.

"You left it to me," she says to the stone. "And that's the end of it. No more words from you."

She crouches down and lays her hand flat against the cool stone.

"Everything is changing," she says. "What do I do now?"

There is no answer.

She sighs.

She waits.

The stone does not answer.

"I do what any mother does," she says finally, bracing her hands on her thighs and rising up. "I save my son."

KING OF CUPS

Qays pays the driver and shuts the door gently, piling his suitcases and telescope case on the curb. The house is dark. Had Nour come here upon her return? What had she told his mother? And why are all the lights off? It isn't that late in the evening.

He leaves his things at the curb and gently slides his key into the lock, trying to come in without sound. He stops at the door for a moment, letting his eyes adjust to the dark. He creeps into the hallway, hearing a voice—his mother's voice. She is reciting something from the Quran.

Her voice travels down the hallway from the kitchen. As he walks down the darkened hallway his eyes are caught by a gleam of light. Looking up, he sees that someone in his absence—Mikayl? His mother?—has placed little phosphorescent stickers of planets and stars along the ceiling of the hallways leading down past the kitchen to the little prayer room.

The door is shut but there is a line of light beneath it. His mother's voice comes from inside.

He gently opens the door, its bottom edge brushing the carpet as it opens.

She is sitting on her prayer rug, her hair covered by a scarf wrapped around it, showing only her face. She looks up when he enters, smiling briefly but returning her attention to the book in front of her, continuing to recite without interruption. He leans against the wall, then slides down it coming to sit cross-legged opposite her.

He waits for her to finish.

When she does, she closes the book and kisses the edge of the pages and places it on the low table in the corner of the small room. "It is a prayer for protection of one's children from evil influences in the world."

He stiffens. "You don't have to pray for me, Ma."

"I wasn't," she says. "I was praying for Mikayl."

He flinches in surprise.

"When Mikayl does bad things he does them because he wants to. He knows I will not approve of them but he doesn't pay attention. Maybe some day he will grow out of that and maybe he won't. Your father drank, you know."

"He did?" Qays asks with surprise. "When?"

"Oh, when we first came to this country. He did. He drank beer. Not anything else. But after you all were born he started to feel bad about it. He wanted to provide a good example, be a good father. He stopped. I wanted him to stop."

"Mama, we're good kids, me and Mikayl. You don't have to be disappointed in us—"

"Disappointed? Me? In you and Mikayl? No, Qays. It is you both who are disappointed in me." She dabs her eyes with her scarf. "You want maybe a real Westernized mother who understands all these changes, who doesn't mind when her son goes to parties and drinks and meets girls."

"Would boys be better?" he blurts out.

She looks sharply at him and opens her mouth to retort, then thinks better of it. "Maybe it would be," she says. "Then I know you are not getting some girl into trouble."

"Getting into a different kind of trouble maybe," he says, trying to get her to smile.

She waves her hand at him in irritation. "Qays, you have to understand, even I had cousins back home who were unmarried. They went off and went about their business and nobody bothered with them. It is a little harder here in America when you want to be so open about it."

"I don't want to be open about it," he says, flustered. Are we even talking about what I think we are talking about? he wondered to himself.

"I wasn't born yesterday," Qamar says. "So I come here and pray."

"For Mikayl," clarifies Qays.

"For Mikayl," she agrees. She draws the letter from her pocket. He sees it and reddens.

"Mama, where did you—"

"You should not have kept this from me," she says quietly. "It was your father's last wishes, *Jaan*. I deserved to see this a long time ago. It was not your place to keep it from me."

He is silent. He wrings his hands. Are there tears in his eyes?

"I don't pray for you, Qays," she says, reaching out and untangling his clenched hands. He won't look at her. "I only pray for myself to be strong enough to be able to be your good mother and help you through whatever hardships may be there in the future for you."

He looks at up her then. He releases his tears. He doesn't understand.

"If I am angry it is because you thought to be afraid to show this letter to me. What kind of a mother have I been that my son could doubt me?"

"Everything is changing, Mama," he says, gasping for breath, his body stiffening with everything he has held inside it for so long. He feels like he has been injured in a thousand places, crushed down against the earth.

This whole time he was dying to breathe and he never knew. He cries harder then, pulling his hands back from her, holding them against his chest.

She comes onto her knees and pulls him against her, hugging him tightly, kissing his face, his hair, his forehead, his ears.

"Now quiet down, *jaan*. Your father knew everything and loved you for it. And now I know everything too, don't I?"

"But what if God doesn't—"

"God is in the sky watching!" she says, batting her hand up at the ceiling. "You let me handle that One! I'll explain everything. I'll make Him see sense! And if He doesn't listen to me then He will listen to your father."

He laughs while he is crying.

"Aren't you still my best little baby boy? Don't you think Mama can take care of everything? I don't understand, Qays. I don't. But I *believe*."

Qays and Qamar both feel the night coming down around them. Qays lies back in his mother's arms, rests his cheek in the crook of her elbow. She begins to sing a little tune.

She is the moon who reflects light down on him.

He closes his eyes.

He sleeps.

THE WORLD

It is a warm evening in Barcelona when Ash hands his ticket to the usher and enters the Palau de la Musica.

What else to do but look toward emptiness as the emptiness of time takes sonic shape?

Horses and lions and other beasts roar sculpturally from the walls. He sits next to a lean man with glittering amber eyes. The lights dim and the conductor emerges to thundering applause.

Ash can feel it radiating through him. The conductor turns to face them, his glossy black hair shining nearly blue and there is a vermilion streak running from his brow up his forehead.

"Strange," Ash says to the man next to him. "My friend told me the conductor tonight was Muslim." The other man looks down into his program to find the name.

Then the violinist strikes the first note and both men forgot themselves, are transfixed by his movement and the sound that emerges.

Alex.

Involuntarily, it seems to Ash, the other man grasps his leg for support and leans forward, listening.

"You know him?" Ash asks the other. "Do you know Alex?"

But the man does not respond. He seems lost in the sound. He has not removed his hand from Ash's leg. Rhythms enter Ash's body through his hand, the floor, the chair.

Then the full chorale of voices enters. Finally Ash can lose himself. He finds himself singing, unable to pronounce any of the words, unsure of the actual tune and feeling the song disappear almost immediately into the air before he can even try to hear it.

But he trusts the endless journeying of the stars above. How many lives have I lived, wonders Ash, where I came here to exactly this place and listened to this moment?

Soon some planet will shift the right way, some star will behave in a way that is until that moment utterly unexpected and then his funny astronomer will be back with all his equipment and star-charts and equations in tow.

Ash is sure of it. He can feel it in his bones.

THE FOOL

Qamar is still sitting there, her back against the wall of the prayer room, Qays drowsing in her arms, when Mikayl and Nour come home and find them.

"Mama, Qays left all his things in the yard," says Mikayl. "Oh Qays, there you are."

"*Batameez,* take your shoes off when you come into the prayer room," Qamar scolds him.

"Sorry, Mama," says Mikayl, sitting down immediately and pulling his sneakers off and tossing them out the door into the hallway where they land with loud clunks.

"Aunty, we just went and bought some groceries," says Nour. "Mikayl thought we should cook a late dinner for you tonight."

She smiles. "That would be nice, dear."

Nour sits down next to Qays. "You had a good trip back?"

He nods. "I'm sorry you didn't stay, Nour. The confluence was magnificent."

"I bet it was," she says with a smile.

"Well, I will show you Venus tonight," Qamar declares.

Qays looked at her with some surprise.

"I too have become an astronomer!" she tells them, with satisfaction.

"Mama," says Mikayl, crawling over to her. He butts her shoulder with his head, like a giant cat.

"Oh God," she says. "I have a big *junglee* boy for a son. Get up," she says to Qays, shifting her arms and pushing him off her knee. "Now you come here," she says and puts her arms around Mikayl. He lies down, resting his head in her lap. She leans down and kisses him on the cheek where she struck him. "Mikayl, *behta…*"

"No, Mama," he says, closing his eyes. "Don't say anything. You don't have to." With his eyes still shut he reaches out and fumbles around, taking Qays' hand and pulls his brother to him. Qays curls up against his brother's body and rests his cheek on Mikayl's chest. "I missed you, Qays," Mikayl mutters, kissing the top of his head. Qays smiles and lifts his brother's hand to his mouth and kisses his knuckles.

"Now I suppose I will have to cook dinner alone," says Nour.

Qamar smiles. "I will help you and these useless boys will help too. But call your father first, *jaan*, and invite him to come over for dinner. I want to talk to him about music."

ABOUT THE AUTHOR

In addition to more than ten volumes of poetry, translations and essays, Kazim Ali is the author of four other books of fiction, *Quinn's Passage, The Disappearance of Seth, The Secret Room: A String Quartet* and *Wind Instrument*. He teaches at Oberlin College in the Creative Writing and Comparative Literature programs.

ABOUT THE PRESS

Sibling Rivalry Press is an independent press based in Little Rock, Arkansas. It is a sponsored project of Fractured Atlas, a nonprofit arts service organization. Contributions to support the operations of Sibling Rivalry Press are tax-deductible to the extent permitted by law, and your donations will directly assist in the publication of work that disturbs and enraptures. To contribute to the publication of more books like this one, please visit our website and click *donate*.

CPSIA information can be obtained
at www.ICGtesting.com
Printed in the USA
FFOW02n0050020916
27330FF